The Cursed Rose

A ROSE IN DARKNESS

HAYLYNN DOWNING

ENTWINED PUBLISHING

A Rose in Darkness
ISBN # 978-1-80250-718-8
©Copyright Haylynn Downing 2025
Cover Art by Kelly Martin ©Copyright January 2025
Interior text design by Entwined Publishing
Published by Eclipse, an Entwined Publishing imprint

Published in 2025 by Entwined Publishing, United Kingdom.

Entwined Publishing is a division of Totally Entwined Group Limited.

Entwined Publishing books by Haylynn Downing

The Cursed Rose
A Rose Among Beasts
A Rose in Darkness

A ROSE IN
DARKNESS

Dedication

This book is dedicated to Cole, without whom I never would have begun writing erotic fiction. Thank you for bullying me into writing that smutty short story for you. Look at where it brought me.

Chapter One

Brielle

Strangers.

"I left another message for your father…I'm sure he'll be here soon."

I hardly register the woman's words as she hovers in front of me, her pink scrubs too vibrant, too happy a color to belong in a night like tonight. My mother. *Our mother…*

"Do you need anything? I can run down to the cafeteria—"

"No." I interrupt her with a stiff shake of my head, refusing to meet her worried gaze as she glances down at my sleeping brother.

"I'll just be in the hallway if you change your mind," she murmurs, her voice quieter but still nicer than I deserve. *She doesn't understand.*

"Brielle? Can I speak to you for a moment?" A man's voice draws my attention to the door, and when I look up, I see the officer from earlier standing there, watching me. I glance over at Sammy, nestled in a cocoon of blankets on the gurney in front of me, and force myself onto numb legs. I shuffle toward him, my irritated eyes burning as we enter the brightly lit hallway. People continue around us, those in scrubs oblivious to the uniformed officer in their midst, while the patients in gowns pause for a moment to stare. I feel myself shifting and stall just outside the door as I spot a well-dressed woman waiting nearby. Her hair is pulled back into a neat bun at the base of her skull, and she's wearing a dress suit, with a white badge hanging around her neck. I can see the writing from here, big red letters that read *Children's Protective Services* with her name, scrawled in black, beneath a photo of her. Susan.

"Hi, Brielle, I'm Suzie." She smiles at me, shuffling the stack of papers in her grasp to one arm so she can extend a hand. Sensing my apprehension, she nods at the officer beside her and takes a small step toward me. "I just wanted to ask you a few questions, if that's all right?"

My eyes track around the room before I realize what I'm doing, my body already involuntarily searching the sea of faces for the one I've been waiting for all night. *Nothing.*

Just more and more strangers.

I slowly turn my attention back to the woman, Suzie, and nod my agreement with a swallow, knowing that, although she's *asking* to speak with me, I don't really have the option of saying no. She gestures to a set of chairs behind me and moves to make herself comfortable in one of the blue plastic seats, but I hover in front of her, my mind drifting back to Samuel.

"I'll go sit with him," the officer, whose name I've forgotten, offers with a tight smile. Again, I don't have the option of declining. He's quick to disappear into the exam room before I can think of a rebuttal, the faint click of the door shutting, sealing my position out here, with another stranger.

"Why don't you have a seat, Brielle?" Suzie smiles up at me, her brown eyes attempting to search mine before I have the chance to drop them to the floor.

"Am...I in trouble?" I whisper, wondering momentarily if being unable to save my mother is punishable by law.

"Why would you be in trouble?" she asks, as if my question is absurd.

I shrug, unsure of how else to answer as I lower myself lethargically into the chair beside her. *I'm exhausted.*

"I'm very sorry for your loss."

Again, I don't reply. What am I supposed to say? I'm sure the standard 'it's okay,' or 'it's not your fault' would suffice, but I've been through too much tonight to expend any more energy trying to console *her*.

"How long was your mother ill?"

Was. Past tense, because she's... I wince and swallow around the lump that's formed in my throat. "Two and a half years."

Truthfully, we'd known something was wrong her entire pregnancy, but it wasn't until after Sammy was born that the doctors discovered the mass growing in her skull.

"That's a long time to live with a terminal diagnosis. How did your family cope?" She jots something down in her notebook and returns her expectant gaze to me, her pen poised against the paper as if already predicting my answer will be worthy of notating.

"W-we just did what we could." I shrug again, unease churning my empty stomach. I'd probably feel nauseated if I hadn't already thrown up everything in my system.

"What about your father? How did he cope?" Her question ignites a surge of anger through my tired brain as if she's just dropped a bomb in my lap, and I become defensive before I even realize where this is going.

"He works a lot to try and pay for her medical bills. What's this about?" I bristle in my chair, pressing my hands together in my lap as I lift my eyes to meet hers.

She sighs and shuffles the papers in her arms, one shoulder rising and falling half-heartedly. "We're just trying to figure out why you were left alone with your three-year-old brother and your severely sick mother... That's a lot of responsibility to place on a child's shoulders."

"I'm seventeen. I'm old enough to be left alone." My rehearsed excuse doesn't seem to sit well with Suzie.

She raises a brow at me and looks up from her notes with a quizzical expression. "Do you know where your father is tonight, Brielle?"

"I already told the officers that he's at work. He has to keep his phone silenced while he's on the clock." *Maybe if I say it enough, it'll be true.*

I know he's *not* at work. If he were, the work boots he'd worn out of the house this morning wouldn't be sitting on the closet floor back at home. I don't know where he is, or what possible explanation he can have for leaving late at night, and dodging every single *fucking* phone call.

"Brielle, we called his job site, and they said he was let go a few months ago."

I blink, unsure if I've heard her correctly. *Let go?* "That's impossible," I whisper as my world tips on its axis. *He was fired?* "He's still getting paid, I've watched him cash the checks."

She shifts, her face falling as if it pains her to see my world come apart at its seams. Where is he? Why wasn't he home? He could've helped.

He could've *saved* her.

"Where are my kids? I want to see my kids!" A familiar voice booms from down the hallway, and when I glance up, I can see my father, shouting at the nurse in the too-happy scrubs by the nurse's station. She's flustered, I can see that from here, her face heating as she crosses her arms over her chest.

"Sir, if you have a seat in the waiting room, I'll have someone come and talk to you—"

"No! I need to see my kids. You can't keep them from me!" He's causing a scene, his voice darker than I've heard it, and his face is puffy from crying. He can't see me, tucked around the corner behind an empty gurney, and although I know I should run to him before he makes things worse, I stay planted in my seat. He backs up, moving away from the desk to a tray of unattended medical supplies, and knocks it over, the loud crashing disturbing the otherwise quiet hospital. People have stopped to watch as he shuffles around, and Suzie is quick to slip from beside me to grab the officer from Samuel's room.

"Well?" My father is seething, jabbing a finger at the other medical staff who've stopped to listen. "Where the hell are they? Samuel? Brielle? Brielle!"

* * * *

"Brielle." A gentle caress along my arm stirs me from my sleep, the nightmarish memory evaporating with each pass of their fingertips against my skin. "Let's get you under the covers."

I open my eyes enough to see Rhys leaning over me, his gaze warming away the chill that's seeped into my bones as he continues stroking a path down my arm. I groan out a weak protest, still exhausted, and furrow my brows as he chuckles and lifts the covers out from beneath my legs, prepared to tuck me in.

"Wait, let me clean her up first." Xander's voice comes from across the room, and it's only now that I realize his gloriously large and naked body is no longer lying beside me. He's standing at the sink in the en suite, his long black curls restrained in a loose ponytail behind his head as his hands work to wring water out of the washcloth in his grasp.

I will never get used to the beauty of these men. I stretch as he crosses toward me, my muscles weak and gelatinous from my climax, and gasp as he runs the warm cloth up my inner thighs, the intrusion making me shiver. He's watching me carefully, his blue gaze intense as he rids me of the stickiness left behind by my arousal, the intimacy of his actions making me flush with embarrassment.

"Amour, are you hurt? You're bleeding."

I glance down as he pulls the cloth away from me, the white now stained with the color of my innocence. I look between the two men, confused. "I-isn't that supposed to happen?"

Xander's face mirrors my own uncertainty, his eyebrows rising in question before his tan cheeks begin to pale and his eyes widen in horror.

"You were a virgin…?" His voice is so low I'm not sure if he's truly searching for an answer, the confusion contorting his features quickly morphing into anger as his steely gaze turns on Rhys. "She was a virgin and you knew. You knew?"

"Xander—" I begin to protest, but my words are cut off by the sound of someone shouting, a slew of curse words filling the otherwise silent home beyond my bedroom door. The guys jump, scrambling for their clothes, but I can't move, my body too tense with surprise and fear. "What is that?

"Stay here with Brielle." Xander barks the order over his shoulder as he rips open the door, his body tensing with unease as another pained shout reaches the top of the stairs.

Everett. *Where is Everett?*

I jump from the bed, grasping for the blanket, and wrap it around myself as I dart around Rhys and into the hallway behind Xander.

"Flower, it's not s—" Rhys' words cut short as he reaches me by the railing, the house falling silent as we stare down at the unconscious and unfamiliar man lying on the floor below us.

Everett is standing over the stranger, huffing, his gun in his grasp as he glares angrily up at his brothers. "Are you going to stand there and stare, or are you going to fucking help me?"

Chapter Two

Everett

Xander is fucking *pissed*.

I can see the anger rippling through him like a tidal wave, the monumental destruction erasing any trace of happiness that had previously lingered in his gaze as it flicks, bewildered, between me and the unconscious man at my feet. Scout Madden, a middle-aged lowlife who peddles drugs and women in his free time, is not only a higher-up on The Wolves' progressive food chain, but also the very man whose name George Beaumont had stashed within our stolen bag of casino chips. *It's too perfect to be a coincidence.* I'm ready to get some fucking answers, and this unlucky bastard is going to give them to me.

"Blaze." My voice is sharp as it cuts through the air, stirring Rhys out of his dumbfounded stupor at the top of the stairs. It's all I can do to avoid the ghostly hazel eyes boring into me, the small, lingering, and fearful whimper that leaves her parted lips causing my jaw to clench angrily as I'm joined at the base of the steps.

Rhys is moving on autopilot, his green eyes clouded with thought as he stoops down to grab the man by his arms, lifting with me so we can begin towing him toward the back of the house. Xander doesn't move until we've disappeared from view, the heaviness of his steps on the stairs nearly drowning out the weak protest that quickly trails behind him.

"Wait, Xander—"

"Go back to your room, Amour. Now!" His harsh order echoes around us as we start down the basement steps, the dank combination of smells forever ingrained in the cement welcoming us back with open arms.

"Where did you find him?" Rhys questions through his teeth, his hands quick to release Scout once we have him positioned where we want him.

"A bar in Brielle's neighborhood." I growl, dropping the man's weight so I can stretch up toward the ceiling. I grasp one of the cuffs dangling from a thick mesh of chain slotted into the ceiling panel, and yank until it releases and lengthens enough for me to ensnare Scout's limp wrists.

"I see she's rubbing off on you, too," Rhys murmurs, a wicked grin pulling up the corner of his lips. He waits, watching until I've secured the man's wrists and have begun pulling him into the air to continue. "Beast's walls are coming down and you...you're finally thinking on your own. Moving on your own orders. It's kinda refreshing, isn't it?"

I roll my eyes and move back a step as Scout begins twitching, the strain of his weight on his wrists stirring him from the unconscious haze holding him under. "F-uck."

I can hear the pain and uncertainty in his voice, the fear lingering beneath his detached mask, and smile, glad that the fucker hasn't had enough alcohol to dull his inhibitions or nerve endings. *I'll be using that to my advantage.* Rhys locks the man into place high enough that his toes barely scrape the floor, and laughs as I move forward to shove the hanging piece of meat hard enough that he swings between us uncontrollably, a low groan coming from the back of his throat.

"Damn!" His swollen eyes flutter and part, just enough for their brown-colored irises to sweep over the brightly lit space in a frenzy, his breathing labored as he spots me in front of him. "You fucking prick."

"Watch it, Madden." Xander's voice booms from behind us, his presence demanding the room. I glance at him over my shoulder and step aside as he stalks closer, a T-shirt covering his previously exposed chest. He's grinning, watching as Scout struggles to balance himself, the black of his eyes enough to chill *me* to the bone.

"What d'you fuckers want?" Scout slurs. His eyes are jumping between Xander and me as if he can't decide which of us he'd rather give his attention to, his body finally stilling in his chains.

"I think the better question is, what do *you* fuckers want? I thought your little gang was smart enough to stay off my fucking toes," Xander growls through his teeth, his arms crossing over his broad chest to showcase the muscle packed onto his body.

"I don' know what you're talking 'bout," Scout grumbles, his angry gaze flicking back over to me. "You got some nerve, jumping me in my own neighborhood."

"If you hadn't been harassing that waitress, we might've been able to chat over a bottle of whiskey." I hiss, stretching out my fingers until the sting in my knuckles returns. I'd punched him so hard in the center of his face that he'd blacked out, and not one fucking person batted an eye when I lugged his unconscious body out to my car. *What did I expect?* No one questioned us when we marched into Beaumont's home and stole his daughter. Why would anyone react differently tonight?

"That bitch was just sore 'cause she didn't get fucked right on her break. I was just offering to — "

He's not allowed to finish his sentence. Xander moves, his fist smashing into Scout's stomach so unexpectedly that the man doesn't have time to prepare. Air rushes from his lungs and sputters past his open lips, his outstretched position ensuring he's unable to catch his breath. I chuckle, relishing the sound of his choking, heaving breaths, and straighten as Xander glares at me over his shoulder, my laughter dying off. He nods toward the fucker dangling in front of us, and backs up, passing me the reins.

This is the opportunity I've been waiting for.

"I'd consider myself a patient man, Scout, but your *pack* is hunting the wrong family. If you know what's good for you, you'll start talking." I almost don't recognize the sound of my voice, the venom in my words darkening it past recognition as I take my brass knuckles out from my pocket. *These men were out to hurt my brother, my girl.* I let the thought buzz around my skull like a pissed-off hornet searching for its target while I slip the weapon over my fist, eyeing Scout. I know where to strike to cause the most damage, the most pain, and when he doesn't immediately answer, I swing. I strike his lower right side, aiming for his liver, and feel a few ribs break beneath the force, the resounding snap of his bones echoing through the cement space. He can only manage a garbled yelp, spit flying past his lips as he sputters and curses, the pain momentarily rolling his eyes to the back of his skull. *Fucker.* I hold out my hand and smile as Rhys passes me his blade, the exposed metal glinting in the overhead light as I hold it up to Scout's contorted face. "Who put the bounty out for us?"

"Go to hell," Scout grunts, feigning a bravery that doesn't meet his panicked eyes.

"You'll be going first." I flash my teeth and grab his shirt, slicing upward into the fabric so it falls away from his fatty, untoned abdomen. He winces, a reaction he's unable to mask, and a low whine of fear drips from his lungs like the sweat trailing down his forehead. I drag the blade across his greasy skin, turning the knife enough to periodically bite into his flesh as I cross his belly and chest. "What do you know about the ambush?"

"I already told ya, fuckers, I don'—" His words morph into a pained cry as I dig the blade of my knife into his pec and slice, splaying the skin of his chest and drawing blood. He curses and tears well as red pools down his stomach, slicking his already wet skin as he writhes in his bindings. *He's going to bleed for every mark on their fucking bodies.* I growl at the memory of Brielle's vacant eyes, the bruises swelling her skin, and the blood pouring from Xander's side. I press the blade into Scout's lower abdomen, prepared to mark him as they marked Xander. I'm only stalled by his strangled laugh and the choked words that follow it.

"W-welcome to the party, Rose."

Chapter Three

Brielle

Four sets of eyes track me as I fumble awkwardly down the last two steps, uncertainty making me clumsy. *What the hell am I doing?* I grimace and push away the question, my eyes defiantly lifting to scan the lion's den as I tread further into the room.

The unknown man is conscious now and dangling, bloodied and bruised, in front of the Grimm Brothers, a sickening familiar grin twisting up his features. Why do I recognize him? Why did he call me *Rose*?

"Flower." Rhys steps in front of me, blocking my view of the scene behind him with his body as he contemplates me with a fierceness I've come to expect from his brothers. "You shouldn't be down here."

I almost nod my agreement. I *know* I shouldn't be down here but, I can't fight the nagging and demanding piece of me that keeps my feet planted on the stained floor. Almost involuntarily I peer around Rhys, taking in the stranger again and the uncanny smile stretched across his familiar face. *I know him.* My eyes jump to the arms bound above his head, to the tattoos covering his biceps, and I stumble backward as my stomach drops with recognition.

"Have you been following me?" The question and the accusation behind it leaves me breathless, my mind racing with memories of that smile haunting my neighborhood. I've *seen* him before—in my neighborhood and by the bus stop, on my way to the library, and outside of Samuel's school. Before my run-in with those men in those woods, I'd believed the howling wolf on his arm to be a beautiful piece of art. Now, it's just the mark of the enemy. "Who the hell are you?"

"Brielle—"

"He wasn't with them in the clearing," I snap, interrupting Rhys, who's unsuccessfully trying to herd me back up the steps. "He's someone else, someone I've seen near my home." I look up at Rhys with urgency, brushing off his hands as they skim my shoulders, and turn, anger boiling through me, to the man hanging in front of us. "What the fuck do you want from me?"

Rhys loops an arm around my waist, prepared to carry me kicking and screaming from the room if necessary, when another low laugh creeps from the man's throat. "It's not what I want, Rose."

Everett lifts the knife to the man's face, his death-like grip around the deadly steel unwavering as he digs the blade into his cheek. "Call her that name one more fucking time, and I'll cut out your goddamn tongue."

"Ya'll a lil' protective of your *toy*?" Despite the threat, and the wound already splitting his chest in an eerie parallel to Xander's injury, the man decides to continue. He rakes his cruel gaze over me, and I can't help the goosebumps that prickle my skin, the

20

sweatshirt and jeans that I'd found and thrown on suddenly not covering enough skin. "You got the sexiest one in —"

Everett doesn't let him finish. His brass-covered knuckles smash into the man's jaw, silencing his words and the laugh that had begun to spill from his split and chapped lips. The man howls, and I jump, a sickening feeling churning my stomach as he spits a stream of blood — and a tooth — to the floor below him.

"Flower, please, go back upstairs." Rhys' low plea pulls my attention away from the slab of meat swinging from the ceiling, his green depths swirling with a mountain of concern I can only withstand for a fleeting moment. I drop my gaze. As much as I'd like to flee to the safety of my room, I have to see this through. I'm a part of this world now. *Their world.*

"Why do you keep calling me Rose?" I question, slipping from Rhys' grasp so I can inch forward, my legs tight beneath me. I stop beside Xander, and hide partially behind Everett's back, praying that their nearness will provide some of the confidence I can feel radiating off them in waves.

"You're more trouble than you're fucking worth." He curses down at me, his words garbled by the blood pooling from the now vacant spot in his gums. He yanks at his chains and growls down at me, frustration and fear flashing in his large eyes. "He's thick in the head for not figurin' that out already."

"Who?" Everett snaps, his patience shredding with each strangled breath the man draws in through his mouth.

"I couldn' point him out even if I *wanted* to help you pricks. I ne'r see him." He rolls his eyes and winces, a moan lashing from his throat as Everett presses the knife into his side, silently threatening to give him another injury to match Xander.

"What kind of dog doesn't know its master?" Everett's skeptical, exasperated expression flickers with excitement as he slowly begins to push his blade forward. The man's skin breaks under the tip of the knife, and a loud shout booms from his chest as he struggles, attempting to put space between himself and the sharp edge beginning to pierce him. "Talk. Now!"

The man doesn't speak, his lips pressing together as if he's resigning himself to the inevitable, and Everett's arm tenses, prepared to deliver a devastating blow.

"Do you know his name?" My voice, although small, stalls each brother in their place, my question tensing their jaws as I, unwittingly, join the interrogation.

I'm not naive enough to believe that this man will live to see another sunrise, to believe that whatever information he provides will prove to be worth his life, but I have to end this. Watching this, and now taking part, is *hurting* me. I can feel my conscious ripping itself to shreds, one piece begging for vengeance and reveling in the injuries Everett is causing, while the other is screaming at him to stop. *This has to end.* The man may not be willing to share his secrets with the Grimm Brothers, but he seems to have a loose tongue where I'm concerned, and I *might* be able to use that to our advantage. Everett withdraws the blade enough for the man to gasp in a lungful of air, and I think for a moment that I can see a change of heart registering on the man's face.

"Course I do. He's the same fuck who offer' your tight little body up as payment to spring you from this place."

I was wrong. That sick smile slides up his face as a chill races through my body, his grin only widening as he senses my discomfort. Xander growls a low, protective sound that rumbles from the back of his throat. He pushes me behind his large frame as if he can shield me from the words that are beginning to spill from the man's mouth. "I heard he's the only one that got out alive. D'you have fun, Ro—"

Now it's Xander who interrupts. His hand is quick to wrap around the man's throat, silencing him before he has the chance to finish his verbal assault, his broken inquiry morphing into a strangled gasp for air that sends me skittering back a step.

"What's the name?" Xander's shout is too loud for the cement space, and I wince, unsurprised to feel Rhys' hands reclaim my waist. He tugs me up, lifting me into his arms, as he turns, determined to get me from the room. I can't pull my eyes away from the scene unfolding behind us, and they water as panic begins to creep onto the unnamed man's face. "What's the fucking name!"

We're up the steps before I have the chance to hear the gargled response, but not far enough to miss the distinct *crunch* that undoubtedly ends his life.

Xander—no, *Beast*—killed him...

"P-put me down." My voice is nothing more than a whisper as I scramble from Rhys' hold, bile burning a fast track up my throat as unwanted images attack me, the man's scared face seared in my brain. I race into the living room, sobbing, desperate, and suffocating. *Air.* I need *air.*

I don't realize that I'm outside until my hands and knees hit the wet grass, my body exhausted and wracked with sobs as I stare up at the early morning light, vomit still threatening to spill from my stomach. *What kind of world is this?* How can these men, these gentle, caring creatures, kill so easily?

I scream.

I scream and I scream until my voice is hoarse and my throat feels raw and desolate. Angry, confused and exhausted, I drop onto the grass, my mind a swirling mess of memories, thoughts and emotions.

"Flower…? Are you okay?"

I glance over to see them all hovering nearby, the Grimm Brothers, my *men*, watching me carefully. An alarm is blaring from inside the house, and guilt swarms me as I realize it must've frightened them when I set it off, their eyes glued to the spot where I lie. "Flower?"

I giggle, surprising them, and myself. *Am I okay?* The question provokes an onslaught of laughter, the sound almost maniacal as it comes from the back of my throat, but I can't seem to stop it from spilling out of my mouth. Of course, I'm *not* okay! Someone is hunting me. Someone with an entire pack of fucking dogs at their disposal, and the only way to stay safe…

I blink, my laughter dying off with my unfinished thoughts. How *will* I stay safe? Once again I find myself scanning the brothers, each one watching me with a warped sense of worry marring their beautiful faces, and I realize then that I have my answer.

The only way to stay safe is by staying with *them.* There's no way I can run from this, no hiding from the gang of men who've mistakenly chased me into my protectors' arms. Three men, who've already proved that they're willing to do what it takes to keep me safe. "No. I'm not okay, but…I think I will be."

* * * *

Lincoln

I'm going to be fucking *rich*.

I smirk and roll my shoulders as Draven, my previously nameless and faceless master, raps his fingers against his desk. He's glowering across the room at the sweating man hovering just inside the office door, the loud bass of the club outside, shaking the walls.

"Was I not clear over the phone? I'm calling your debt, George. *All* of your debt." Draven's voice matches his eyes. Cold and emotionless, they pin the trembling man in place as his shaking fingers riffle through the wad of cash in his grip. He's re-counting it, hoping, praying, that a few thousand dollars will magically appear in the stack. He can count it as many times as he wants. There will never be enough.

"Please, Draven, if I could —"

"Mr. Augustin," Draven corrects, and I snicker, relishing in the power behind that name, the *money* behind that name. I'm going to be *so fucking* rich.

"Mr. Augustin, I'm sorry. I-I just didn't have enough time," George whispers, his head dropping so his eyes fall to his scuffed shoes. He's wearing an oversized button-down shirt and faded black slacks, as if dressing up would somehow earn him Draven's favor. The poor son of a bitch still doesn't know. This has nothing to do with *him*.

"You didn't have enough time? Was six years not an ample enough window for you?" Draven stands, his anger palpable as he rounds the desk, sizing up the broken and defeated man across from him as he leans back against his desk. "I paid, out of my pocket, for every hospital visit, every round of chemo, and bottle of medication for your *wife*, and you dare to fucking stand there, defaming my generosity?" George winces but doesn't respond. Even I know that it's a low blow, but the man should know better than to retaliate against Draven fucking *Augustin*. "You know, I'm a reasonable man, George, and I love a good bargain. Maybe there's something you can offer me that's worthy of my time…something that may persuade me to forgive your debt entirely."

George's face pales in disbelief, and he stumbles forward in shock. "What is it? Please, just name it, and it's yours."

"I want Brielle."

I try not to look confused at the name he's used for the girl, and instead, focus on the way George's mouth opens and closes like a fish out of water. I snort.

"Brielle…?" It's as if George hasn't fully registered the request, his mouth still parted in utter horror.

"You asked me to waste my time and resources to rescue her, so I thought it only fair that once she's freed, she comes home to *me*." Draven's eyes are alight with fire as his mind wanders to his target. His *Rose*.

"No. I'm not going to sell you my fucking daughter." The thought perturbs George enough that he throws the cash in Draven's face, whatever fear had momentarily stalled him by the door lifting. He storms forward, and Draven snaps his fingers, ordering me to move.

I am getting my damn money.

I shove my hands into George's chest, pushing him back hard enough that he nearly falls on his ass.

"It's a shame you couldn't see things my way, George. Your children would've been better off." Draven chuckles, wiping away the invisible dirt the man's money has tarnished him with.

"You leave my children out of this! This is between you and me." George is shaking, his hands balling into fists as if he's ready to strike.

Do it, old man. Fucking do it! I bring my knee up into his ribs, breaking them and sending him to the floor as Draven laughs from behind us.

"Not anymore, George. Now, this is between me and Rose."

Chapter Four

Xander

It's been three days since I killed Scout Madden. I'm counting, because in the three days since his death, I've been unable to locate Lincoln *fucking* Fisher.

I growl and press a hand to my temple, grimacing as a headache throbs through my skull, incessant and unrelenting like the phone buzzing in my pocket. I resist the urge to check it, knowing that if they'd managed to find something, anything, worth mentioning, they'd call. These texts are simply notifying me that there's been no change, a taunting reminder that despite our efforts, we're still coming up empty-handed. I smash my fist against my desk, rattling the nearly emptied glass of whiskey I'd been sipping from, and growl as a knock sounds at my office door.

"What?" I bark, forcing in a short, steadying breath as Everett pushes into the room, looking as fatigued and defeated as I feel. Even with the extra hands that

I've hired to help in the hunt for Lincoln, my brothers and I are still overburdened and struggling to keep up with the demands running our empire has placed on us. We've been rotating in shifts, one brother leading the search party, while the other two tend to our businesses and Brielle. It's exhausting, but her safety is more important than a few hours of missed sleep.

He sits in the chair across from my desk and eyes the glass of whiskey in my grasp as I lift it to my lips, a questioning look lifting his brow. "Don't start. I know it's early."

"How much longer are you planning on avoiding Brielle?"

I can't help but wince at his brashness, this new, outspoken, and authoritative version of Everett, still taking some time to get used to.

"I'm not avoiding her," I growl, and grab the nearby decanter so I can refill my glass. I've never run from *anything* in my life before, but... "I just can't see her right now."

"Why?" His brown eyes are scanning me so intensely that I feel like he's trying to find the answer telepathically, concern and confusion masking his tired gaze.

I almost tell him to fuck off, that automatic and involuntary reaction programmed into my core. I've been beaten and trained to *never* show any weakness, so sitting here now, contemplating talking about the thoughts in my fucked-up mind, is making me uneasy. I toss back the glass of liquor and refill it again before I respond. "I've tarnished her, Everett. I can't...I *need* to be better for her first."

"If this is about taking her virginity—"

"It's not just about that." I pause, knowing that, truthfully, I *do* have regrets about that night but, despite the progress I've made, I'm still not ready to delve that far into my thoughts with him. "I've exposed her to so much death. I've shown her what we — what I — am truly capable of, and I'm worried." I hesitate again, hating the vulnerability sharing is making me feel. "I'm worried I'm not good enough."

I whisper the last bit, grimacing as a twinge of self-consciousness bites through my boosted ego. I pull another long sip from my glass, relishing in the delicious burn that tracks down my throat, and sigh, my body tense. I feel like a bug beneath a microscope, Everett's attentive eyes wide as he finally glimpses the mess of hurt, pain, and fear that darkens my thoughts.

His face has fallen, a frown pulling down the corners of his lips as he thinks over my response, his dark brows drawn low over his eyes. "Xander, you did what you had to do to protect her."

His words do little to console me.

"What I *had* to do is making her lose sleep. You can't tell me she's fucking okay right now," I snap, angry with no one other than myself. *With Beast.*

"Of course she's not okay, Xander, she just found out that the pack of men who tried to abduct her have also been stalking her for god knows how fucking long. Shutting her out isn't going to fix anything. This is bigger than you, this is bigger than all of us."

I hate that he's right. I hate that sitting here and talking to him is *helping*. This isn't what I was raised to do, or who I was raised to be. This isn't the *Beast* my father created.

"You should go see her. She's going to need all of us to get through this."

He stands, stretching his arms above his head as he yawns and starts toward the door, sated. I think he's going to leave, having said his peace, but he pauses halfway and glances back at me over his shoulder, his exhausted eyes light as he scans me.

"You're trying, Xander. We see you." He doesn't stay around to see the reaction that his words cause, slipping through the door as silently as he'd entered.

I feel like I can't breathe, my chest tight with emotion as a small flicker of light sparks through my chest. I cling to the hope that follows in the wake of his promise, relishing in it. *Maybe I don't have to be the Beast he made.*

"I can't," I mutter, the thought evaporating as quickly as it had formed. No one can change *that* much.

An email from David pings across the computer and I growl, defeated by the lack of news it divulges. When I discovered Lincoln was connected to this mess, I pulled David off the task of locating Brielle's missing information in favor of having him track our new target, instead. Well, attempting, to track our target.

Lincoln.

Fucking.

Fisher.

For as idiotic as the man must be to have flunked the same grade four times, he's been clever enough to stay off the fucking grid. He's not used a single credit card, computer, or traceable phone since the attack, and he's not been spotted in any local bars or motels. I'd hoped in my blind rage that *maybe* I'd struck the son of a bitch with a stray bullet, but there's been no reports of a GSW at any of our local hospitals.

If I'm lucky, he's dead.

If I'm unlucky?

I cringe. If I'm unlucky, then his IP address and other personal information is being stowed away somewhere. Like Brielle's and her brother's has been. But by who? There isn't a hacker in this city with more skill than David and, if there were, The Wolves wouldn't be able to afford them on their shitty payroll.

I roll my shoulders and lift my glass to my lips to finish off the remaining liquor. My eyes drift to the door, and my thoughts unravel until only one thing remains. Brielle. I know I need to go and see her, but I can't help the unfamiliar bite of fear that keeps me planted my chair. *What if she doesn't want to see me?* It's been three days. Three days for her to grow unforgiving of my murderous outbursts, and resentful toward me for taking her innocence. I can't possibly face her but, as I look through my crystal tumbler toward the door sealing me in my solitude, I realize that I don't have a fucking choice. I *have* to see her. I need to know where we stand.

I'm moving before the thought has even finished forming in my mind, my body only stalling once I cross the threshold into her bedroom. It's dark, and I blink, my eyes slow to adjust to the dim lighting as a solid force hits my chest, knocking the air from my lungs. I wince, unprepared for the arms that wrap around my waist or the head that buries against my chest.

"Xander..." Brielle's soft voice cracks my chest open, a shaky sigh of contentment leaving her lips as I pull her tighter against me. We stand like that for a painstakingly long time in silence, embracing one another as if we're too afraid to speak or let go.

"Amour, I'm sorry," I whisper, speaking the words I'd believed to have been beaten from my vocabulary a long time ago.

"No more shutting me out, okay?" She looks up at me, and I cup her face, my thumb rubbing delicately over the bruise still darkening her skin.

"I promise I'm trying." As honest as my answer is, I know it isn't good enough. *I'm* not good enough. She leans into my touch, her hazel eyes lifting to meet mine, and I frown at the dark circles swelling the skin beneath them. "You need to sleep."

My stern order makes her sigh, her eyebrows furrowing as she chews on her lower lip. I glance over toward the bed and spot Rhys tucked beneath the mountain of blankets, one arm stretched toward her empty side as if searching for her warmth. He and Everett have been sleeping in here with her, attempting to comfort her enough with their presence to lull her to sleep, but the bags beneath her eyes are proof that it's not been working. I don't need to ask why she hasn't been sleeping. I know that every time she closes her eyes, the faces of those men come back to haunt her, their deaths, no matter how deserving, blemishing her soul. *You never forget witnessing your first murder.*

"I have some pills that can help."

She blinks at me, her lips pursing as the urge to argue rises. Thankfully, her exhaustion placates her, and the words that had been forming are erased by the large yawn that contorts her features. I nod toward the bathroom, my hands slow to release her as I take a step away from her. "Why don't you go hop in the shower, and we'll lie down once you're out?"

She glances toward the bathroom and nods, compliantly crossing the room, her brown waves tangled and tied into a sloppy ponytail at the base of her neck. I watch her go, my eyes sweeping over my brother's sleeping form before I slip from the room.

I'm able to scramble up the bottle of sleeping pills, a glass of water, Everett, and a thick hoodie from my closet before she's out of the shower. When she emerges from the bathroom, wearing my sweatshirt and a thick pair of socks, her wet hair is braided down the back of her head and she looks almost sickly, the bags beneath her eyes and the bruises on her skin a stark contrast to her pale complexion. Despite the exhaustion weighing her down, she seems surprised — and *happy* — to see all three of us lying in her bed. Rhys is still half-sleep, only having roused enough to make room, and Everett has plopped down beside me with an arm bent beneath his head, his brown eyes tracking Brielle as she scurries across the room.

She pauses beside the bed to take the two pills lying on the nightstand and finishes the water before yawning and climbing in beside us. She's clumsy and sluggish, and I can't help the awkward, unpracticed laugh that leaves me as she lies down between us and scoots toward me. I wrap an arm around her waist and tug her into my chest as Everett spoons her from behind, her body relaxing as her face nuzzles into the crook of my neck. *This is what she needed.*

"We're here, Amour." I press my lips to her forehead and bury my face in her hair, inhaling the sweet honey scent that floats up from the wet strands. "You're safe."

She's no match for the medication that works through her system, her heavy eyes shutting soon after she's stilled in my grasp. Everett grins sleepily from behind her, his fingers tracing her arm as he begins to drift, a small thank-you floating from him with a yawn. I nod even though he can't see it and stroke a thumb over Brielle's parted lips, savoring the feel of their warmth against my skin. She's so small like this, curled into my side, tucked in between my brother and me...so vulnerable and defenseless. The stress of these past few days has disappeared from her body, and I relish how peaceful she looks, asleep, content and protected. She is going to need all of us to get through this, *all* of us, and I'll be damned before I withhold myself for one more fucking second.

Chapter Five

Brielle

I'm disoriented when I wake.

My bed is empty, the three large bodies that had previously bracketed me in place, gone. I sit up, my head spinning from the movement, and glance around the room, my eyes falling on the light spilling in from behind the curtains. The sun is high enough for it to be afternoon and despite having only slept for around five hours after three all-nighters, I feel surprisingly rested and *awake*.

Untangling the thick blankets from around my waist and legs, I push myself up and start toward the closet, my feet unsteady beneath me. The once bare space has been filled with clothes, each item hung from a velvet hanger, organized by color, and grouped with like items. There's a section for T-shirts, blouses, jeans, dresses and drawers filled with lingerie, underwear, bras and socks. Honestly, it's all a bit overwhelming—

a gift from Rhys I haven't had time to fully explore yet. I've never owned anything as luscious as the fabrics that fill this space, and I've certainly never had a closet full of clothes to fuss over.

I do my best to work through the pieces quickly, settling on a pair of jeans and a cropped graphic T-shirt. Forgoing any socks or shoes, I cross through the bedroom barefoot, my fingers working to tame the messy plait of hair braided down the back of my head as I step into the hall.

It's quiet, an uncanny normalcy I still struggle to adjust to. Scanning the hallways on either side of me, I cross my arms around my body, an unwanted bout of fear skittering up my spine as I worry, involuntarily, that I've been left here alone. I know that my fear is irrational—the brothers, despite their unyielding search for my nameless threat and the demands of their amassed empire, have always ensured that I'm not left unprotected. Someone is always here, researching, resting, or attempting to coax me to sleep. Still, even with this knowledge, anxiety continues to wrap its gangly fingers around me, ensnaring me until it's difficult to breathe. The grip of its bone-like fingers is only broken by the sound of a shower turning on down the hall to my left, and I rush toward it, adrenaline making my heart flutter in my chest.

I pass Rhys' room in a hurry, skittering down the hall until I'm standing in front of the door to Everett's en suite. Music is pooling out from beneath the door, a disjointed, classical ensemble that resonates through the bare space and masks the sound of the door closing behind me as I slip into the bathroom. Steam is spilling in tendrils from the shower, the glass door so clouded with it that Everett's figure is blurred and distorted behind it. I have no intention of interrupting him, but my feet move subconsciously beneath me, carrying me across the slick tile and to the edge of the shower. Without thinking, I pull open the door and peer in at him, watching in wonder as the water cascades over his face and down his body. *Fuck.* Just like his brothers, this man is a perfect specimen of the male species, the sight of his thick cock enough to curl my stomach with need and desire.

"Hello, pet." Everett's deep voice startles me, my eyes snapping away from the erection growing between his legs to the searing brown gaze that's scanning me. I flush, my face heating with embarrassment as I tuck my lower lip between my teeth, ashamed to have been caught staring. "I thought I heard you."

"I-I didn't mean to pry, I just…" I trail off, unsure of the reasoning behind barging in on his shower. Was it curiosity? Fear? *Lust?* I swallow, and scan his brown eyes again, their intense color heated, but clouded with his undeniable exhaustion. They've all been working so tirelessly…for *me.*

"Did you want to join me, pet?" His husky invitation makes a shiver race up my spine, but I gratefully accept his offer, my fingers slow and graceless as I peel the clothes away from my curvy frame. His breath stalls in his chest as I kick off my panties, a moan of appreciation bubbling from his throat as his eyes rake over my exposed body.

He's watching me hungrily, and as I settle into the stall with him, I find myself determined to make this showering experience more pleasurable than our last. I grab the rag hanging beside me and hold it up into the space between us, a suggestive smile curling onto my lips.

"Can I wash you?" My question makes his cock jump, his nostrils flaring as a possessive growl slips past his parted lips.

He nods, his hands skimming across my skin as I reach forward to snag his body wash off the shelf, his eyes not once leaving mine as I lather the rag and press it against his chest. I drag it along his skin, the movement once again teleporting me back to the night that he washed and erased my attacker's blood from my body. *Can I do the same for him?* Free him from—or at least relieve a bit of—the pressure weighing him down?

Tucking a stray strand of hair behind my ear, I drop to my knees and eye him with mischief as I race the cloth over his erect cock. He bites back a groan and presses his hips forward, thrusting his dick harder into my grasp as I smile up at him innocently.

"Are you teasing me, pet?" He grits through his teeth, a smile pulling onto his lips as I drop the cloth to scrub his feet.

"Never, *sir*," I muse, loving the dangerous grin that slices across his face at my remark.

He moves so quickly that I'm almost unprepared for the cold tile of the shower wall as I'm pressed against it, his large body pinning me in place from behind. A squeak of surprise escapes me and I press back, trying to alleviate the chill that's pebbled my nipples.

"Did you forget your warning, Brielle?" The heat of his words caresses the shell of my ear before his teeth sink into my shoulder, that quick prick of pain sending a spike of pleasure straight to my core. I groan, my eyes rolling back as he presses his hard cock against me, tempting and teasing me, provoking me as I had him.

"I didn't forget." His previous message echoes through my head, and I bite into my lower lip as I peer over my shoulder at him.

"So, you coming down into the basement was a direct act of disobedience and not a simple mistake? Interesting, pet." He swats my ass, hard enough that the resounding sound reverberates through the stall, and I yelp. "I'm sorry, sir." I try to appear guilty, my lips turned down in a mock pout as I grind my ass into him, desperate to distract him at least for a few minutes. He hisses, his hands quick to grip my waist in an attempt to still me as his words fall hot onto my skin.

"You're playing with fire, Brielle." He warns, his voice low, and dangerous. He smacks my lifted ass again and tugs at my braid, tilting my head to the side so he can kiss down the length of my neck. "I ought to bend you over my knee for interrupting us."

"I know my safewords," I moan out, shivering as his tongue trails over a tender section at the base of my shoulder.

At my invitation, he shuts the water off and pulls me into his arms, our wet bodies slick against one another as he carries me into his bedroom, chuckling. He drops me onto the bed and crawls up my wet, naked body, his chest sliding along mine as he leans over me with a grin.

"What you did was dangerous, pet. I will not tolerate you continuing to put your life at risk," he warns, his hand slipping between my thighs.

"You three were there to protect me," I whisper, defending my actions as if I want to change the punishment I know is coming.

"And if he'd managed to steal one of our guns and kill us all? You walked in there without thinking, Brielle," he scolds, his fingers parting my folds, caressing me as I spread my legs open further for him.

I know that he's right. I *was* being careless, but despite agreeing with him, I push anyway, desperate to provide him a moment of reprieve. "I'd have heard the fight or the gunfire."

He growls and pushes two punishing fingers into me, slamming hard into my pussy until a low whimper rushes past my lips.

"You may be willing to throw caution to the wind, but I will not be so careless with your well-being. You'll learn to think twice before making that mistake again." His threat makes me shiver, his fingers slow and tantalizing as they slip from me, soaking wet with my desire. He circles my clit, drawing small whimpers of pleasure from my throat as his other hand reaches up to cup my breast, his thumb tracing over my hard nipple delicately. If his punishments continue to be this pleasurable, I'm not sure I'll ever behave again.

He dips a finger back into me and curls up, pressing along my wall and sending a delicious spark of pleasure through me so overwhelming my hips buck off the bed. I cry out, my eyes squeezing shut as his lips close around my free nipple, his delectable touch nearly causing me to explode around him. He pauses his ministrations just as my orgasm begins to crest over the mountain, and I cry out, desperate to continue my climb. "Everett, please!"

"Feel good, Brielle?" he whispers, slowly beginning to circle me again. I moan, dropping my head back against the pillow as the intense feeling comes back, nearly tipping me over the edge.

"Yes!" I shout, riding his fingers as he presses against the sensitive bundle of nerves within me, my entire body tense with the orgasm threatening to detonate through me.

"Good." He kisses my temple, and again, as my body is about to convulse around him with completion, he stops.

"W-wait, what? Everett—"

"I warned you, pet." He smirks, and I frown, only now realizing that he'd *purposefully* denied me my orgasm.

"Fuck." I curse, frustration blooming in my chest as he sucks his fingers into his mouth, licking them clean of the desire that had soaked them. "Sir, please."

I scramble to my knees and wrap my arms around his neck, my entire body aching and *wanting* as I press my lips to his neck, kissing a trail up to his jaw, desperate.

He laughs, and pries my arms from around him, shaking his head. "No, Brielle. This is your punishment."

"Please, I didn't mean—"

He shakes his head again and stands, leaning over so he can tuck a finger beneath my chin as I pant. "I've got to do my rounds, soon. I should only be gone for a few hours, but if you can manage to *behave* while I'm out, I'll reward you when I get home."

I scowl at him, understanding what he's ordering without having to ask for clarification. *No orgasms.* I chew on my bottom lip, upset, tense, and needy, but I don't argue, satisfied with the light glinting in his eyes. My plan is working. *He's distracted.*

"I'll be good, sir. I promise."

Chapter Six

Rhys

She's awake. Eating. *Smiling.*

I lean against the couch, watching in astonishment as Brielle lifts another sugary bite to her mouth, a small tune humming past her lips as she chews happily.

Mrs. Claebourne is bustling around the kitchen, cleaning up the pancake batter splattered along the counter, and she winks when she spots me, nodding in satisfaction as Brielle takes a long sip of her coffee.

"Flower." I can't stop myself from moving toward her, desperate to feel the warmth of her skin. I reach her at the island and skim my hands along her waist, taking her in as she stares up at me through her eyelashes, her hazel eyes heated despite the stress tensing her shoulders. "How're you feeling?"

"I feel good. It's amazing what some caffeine and a few hours of sleep can do," she murmurs, a soft smile curling her lips as she works to cut another bite of food.

The bags underneath her eyes have lightened, and the rosy tint has returned to her pale cheeks. She's wearing a T-shirt and jeans, an outfit I purchased for her, and her brown hair cascades over her shoulders in tight waves. I brush a hand along her cheek, my fingers skimming the bruise still yellowing her skin, and sit down beside her, as my stomach twists with disgust at the memory.

"A few *days*, you mean." My correction is gentle, but the words are still enough to stall her mid-bite. Her hazel eyes flick back up to me, her lips parted in a silent curse.

"Days? I've been asleep for a few *days*?" she questions, the rosy color I'd been admiring just a few moments before vanishing from her cheeks.

"You needed the rest, Flower, and, unfortunately, you haven't missed anything," I state, hating the panic that settles onto her face.

In the week since Scout Madden provided Lincoln's name, we've searched every bar, casino, apartment, hotel and neighborhood in the surrounding area. The man seems to have disappeared, but we're not naive enough to believe that the threat to Brielle's safety has disappeared with him. We've hired additional security to monitor our property, and men now escort each of us to and from our home. Xander still believes that George is somehow involved in all of this, and while Everett doesn't disagree that Lincoln has a puppet master, he's not ready to place the blame solely on Brielle's father. Me, I'm not sure where I stand. I'd like to sit down and talk to Beaumont, but he and the brother Brielle cries about in her sleep haven't turned up on our radar yet, either. They've all just...*vanished.*

"Is there anything I can do to help?" Brielle asks softly, her food forgotten in front of her.

"No, Flower. We're handling it." I shake my head, a piece of me tearing in two as I watch a battle of emotions wage on her features. I want to tell her that her family is missing. I want to tell her that we have the name of the man responsible for the attack in the clearing. I want to tell her that he's gone too, but I *can't*. She's still too fragile. We've agreed that until her mental and physical status improves, we can't involve her any further. We will *not* break her. "We're going to keep you safe, Brielle. I promise."

"I know." She nods, swallowing forcefully in an attempt to clear her throat. She shakes away whatever thought is clouding her head, and glances back down at her coffee, picking it up and sipping from it as she watches me. "I interrupted Everett's shower this morning."

I'm surprised by the change in topic, but I welcome the confession with a laugh. "Yeah? How did that go?"

She glances around the room, ensuring Mrs. Claebourne isn't within earshot, and leans close.

"Fine, until I learned that orgasm denial was a thing," she quips, raising a brow at me in question as if *I* had something to do with Everett's choice of punishment.

I chuckle as I lean into her, watching as she squirms in her chair, her face beginning to heat with need. "Maybe if you'd behave, my brother wouldn't have to punish you."

I nip her lobe and she shivers, a small whimper chasing past her lips on a sigh. I swallow back a groan, inhaling her delicious scent as she parts her thighs and leans forward, overwrought by her body's demands.

"I'll break all of his rules if it means he gets a break," she whispers as she slips from her chair, not allowing me a moment to contemplate her words. "I haven't had the chance to thank you for my new clothes. Can I try them on for you?"

I gape at her question, an understanding settling over me as she glances over her shoulder at me with a smile. *She wants to give us all a break.* We won't allow her to aid in the search, so she's finding her own way to lend a hand. *She's distracting us.*

I nod and hold out my hand for her to take, allowing her to lead me up the stairs and to her room. I can see the excitement growing in her eyes, the color returning to her cheeks, and I smile as she disappears into her closet to try on the first set of clothes. If *this* is what it takes, just a small amount of our time, to bring her back to life? Then she can have every fucking minute of the rest of my existence.

Chapter Seven

Brielle

"Holy fuck, Flower." Rhys groans, the tortured and guttural sound coming from the back of his throat as I turn slowly in front of him. I'm modeling one of the dresses he's purchased for me—a red satin skintight mini that clings to and displays every available inch of my curvaceous body, the little scrap of fabric leaving nothing to the imagination. The neckline is deep, plunging to the upper part of my abdomen, and the skirt is short, barely brushing the tops of my thighs with a slit that stretches up to my right hip. Paired with an open back, it guarantees that I go bare underneath, a temptation not only for my men but for me, too. "You're gorgeous, Brielle. Stunning."

I chew on my lower lip, embarrassed by his words. It doesn't matter that he's seen me naked or that he watched while I was fucked into oblivion a few days prior, his compliments will always feel so...so *intimate*.

"The clothes are beautiful, Rhys. I can't thank you enough."

"You don't have to thank me, Flower, it's the least I could do. If Xander hadn't been so impulsive, he might've remembered that you'd need something to wear." Rhys rolls his eyes, an annoyed expression flicking across his face as he, no doubt, remembers the first time that we met. I was slung over Xander's shoulder like a pack of meat, cursing, flailing and bleeding. I still don't understand why he hadn't been there that day, but I know better than to lose myself to the *what-ifs* and *could-bes*.

"Is he mad at me?" I'm unable to stop the question that floats past my lips at the thought of Xander, my mysterious and bad-tempered protector. I knew that he'd been avoiding me since that night in the basement — *the night that he claimed my virginity* — but I didn't know and I couldn't understand why. I wanted to ask him. I wanted an explanation. I'd planned on demanding a fucking *answer* from him but...when the time finally came, I was too exhausted to try.

"Who? Xander?" Rhys is adjusting the bulge straining against his jeans, his eyebrow raised in confusion as I disappear into the closet to change. "Why would he be mad at you?"

"I think he's been avoiding me. Or, at least he was before I fell asleep," I call, sighing as I slip back into the jeans and T-shirt I'd picked earlier this afternoon. My stomach is still coiled uncomfortably from my punishment and my core throbs incessantly with need, but I can't act on my desires just yet. *I have to behave.*

I race my hands through my waves and step back into the bedroom, my chest tightening as I shrink beneath Rhys' steady gaze. He tilts his head to the side and sighs, his hand lightly tapping his thigh in invitation. "Come here, Flower."

I cross the room toward him, shivering as his hands skim my waist, his long fingers wrapping around my hips so he can gently tug me into his lap. I lean my head against his chest, greedily breathing in the spicy aroma of his skin.

"Why is he angry at me?" I glance up at him through my lashes, afraid to hear his answer.

I can see him contemplating his response, his jaw moving as he chews on the inside of his cheek. "He overthinks everything, Flower. His life has been, well...*difficult* would be an understatement. You should talk to him, Brielle. He's not angry with you, he's just beating himself up."

He doesn't delve any further and I know that, even if I keep prodding, I'll be met with the same response. Rhys knows as well as I do that the only person who can explain what's going on inside Xander's head, is *Xander*. I have to talk to him.

I stifle a yawn and nuzzle into the crook of Rhys' neck, exhaustion still an unwelcome and hovering guest. It seems that, despite the forty-eight hours of uninterrupted sleep, I'm still not fully recovered from the all-nighters my nightmares had forced me to pull earlier this week.

I tense in Rhys' grasp, one final, nagging question floating to the front of my mind. "That man that Everett brought here. Did he give up a name before...?" I trail off, unwilling to finish the sentence. Before *Beast* killed him.

"Flower, I really don't think—"

"I *know* you three are intent on keeping me at arm's length with this, but it's *my* mess," I interrupt defensively, pulling back enough that I can meet his worried gaze.

He scans me as if attempting to gauge me for a reaction to the response he hasn't provided, yet. "Lincoln Fisher."

I wait for the name to spark some sort of recollection, maybe a deep, recessed memory buried somewhere within the recesses of my brain, but there's nothing. *Nothing.*

"Lincoln Fisher," I repeat, surprised by the tears that sting and blur my vision. I don't know why I'd hoped to know the man — after all, isn't it better that I don't? — but an overwhelming sense of grief comes at the realization that he's a *stranger*. A stranger intent on claiming me. For what? For himself? For someone else? Why? *Why!*

"Brielle." Rhys' soft voice brings me back, and I have to force back the tears before they have the chance to fall. *I can't cry.* I've cried enough over this.

"It's nice to have a name for his face," I murmur. A name for the face that haunts me. A name for the *monster* that survived. I shake my head, refusing to be a black cloud that plagues the men who are so hellbent on keeping me safe. I force out a breath and put a smile on my face, desperate to remain positive. "Do you think I could make dinner tonight?"

Rhys raises a brow at me but doesn't question the sudden change in topic, like he hadn't earlier. I know it's not a healthy coping mechanism, constantly ignoring my fears, but for now, it's all I can do to keep myself from falling apart. *That, and taking care of them.*

"What did you have in mind?" Rhys presses a kiss to my forehead, his hand stroking comfortingly down my back.

"I'll have to see what food we have first," I quip, thinking of all the recipes my mother taught me before she'd started getting sick.

"I can help. I do know my way around the kitchen." He chuckles, proud to be the only one, aside from Mrs. Claebourne, who can manage to make a good meal.

"I'm sure you know your way around a lot of things," I tease as I press a kiss to his cheek, standing as his erection begins to push against my ass. He tries to reach for me, intent on keeping me in his arms, but I'm too quick, making my way toward the bedroom door before he can lure me into misbehaving.

"I'd like to learn my way around you," he calls after me seductively, winking when I turn to meet his heated gaze.

"I'm being punished, remember? I'm not allowed to come before Everett gets home." I pout, a shock of pleasure bolting straight to my core as he watches me, his tongue slow to drag along his bottom lip.

"How would he know?" he whines, an exasperated look crossing his face. I giggle at his dismay, pleased that someone *else* is being tortured with me, but I stop when I feel a hard chest against my back.

"I'd know." Everett's gravelly voice makes me whimper, a shiver of desire skittering up my spine as he leans into me, his fingers tracing delicately over my jaw as he addresses Rhys. "I'd smell her arousal on your fingers. On your breath." He turns so I'm facing him, his hand wrapping around the back of my neck so he can pull me closer. "My brothers may have rushed to sink their cocks into you, but I'm a patient man, Brielle. He may still need to learn your body, but I know what makes you come. I know what makes you scream."

I moan and he growls out a sound of approval, his brown eyes searing as they stare into mine.

"On your knees, pet. You've been good, and I think you deserve a reward."

Chapter Eight

Everett

I smile in satisfaction as Brielle drops gracefully to her knees, a mischievous look lighting up her otherwise pale features as she stares up at me. *Fuck, she's breathtaking.* I reach out and caress her hair, stroking the tight waves as Rhys shifts beneath my gaze, an apologetic smile curling up the corner of his lips as I eye him.

"Trying to tempt my pet into disobeying my orders, Rhys?"

He rolls those green eyes, attempting to look indifferent or *unaffected* by the consequences he knows his actions could bring, but the tightening of his jaw and the quickening of his breath gives him away. My hand pauses in Brielle's hair, and I chuckle at his outward defiance, my head tilting as I level him with my gaze.

"Keep it up. You may be my brother, Blaze, but you are *not* above being punished."

Brielle's attention, having wandered to follow our conversation, snaps back to me, a curious and questioning look quirking her brow as Rhys stands to leave.

"You can't fault me for trying. She's too damn tempting to keep my hands off of." He smirks wickedly as he starts toward us, wanting to stay and play, but understanding without my having to ask that I want time alone with her. I nod my thanks as he stoops down in front of Brielle, his fingers brushing away a stray lock of her hair before they trail down to trace her lips. "What a good submissive you're turning out to be, Flower."

She blushes, her mouth parting in a silent moan as his thumb traces along her bottom lip, her body shivering as his touch sparks her desires to new heights. It's as he's dropping his hand away from her that she reaches out and nips his finger, the unexpected and erotic action causing a low groan to ripple from the back of his throat. I can see the hesitation tensing his body as he stands, reluctant to leave this tantalizing woman alone with me, but he concedes, muttering under his breath that I'm a *lucky bastard* as he goes.

I wait until the door has closed behind him to step away from her, taking a moment in the silence to admire her position on the floor. She's fucking glorious kneeling by my feet, her lips and thighs parted as she pants in anticipation, waiting for my next command. So. Fucking. *Perfect*.

"Would you like to pick your reward, pet, or would you like me to choose it for you?" My voice is ragged with lust, and I feel my cock jump in my pants as I momentarily lose what little control I have over myself in her presence.

Her eyes are clouded as she scans me, and her tongue is slow to drag across her lips, wetting them while she contemplates her answer. Finally, she responds. "I want to taste you."

Fucking hell. It's almost impossible to keep the shocked expression off my face, my breath catching in my throat as she scoots toward me, her lower lip trapped between her teeth as she awaits my answer. Of all the possible things this woman could've asked for…that request is *not* one I'd planned on hearing.

"You want me in your mouth, pet?" I whisper, gesturing her forward with the crook of my finger. She's quick to move, crawling on her hands and knees until she's closed the small distance between us and is kneeling by my feet again, a small whimper brushing past her lips.

"Please, sir?" She lifts her hands toward my zipper hesitantly, her movements slow, thought out, and calculated. *She's giving me time to reject her.* As if I'd deny her, deny *myself*, of this reward.

"Yes, pet," I murmur, twisting a strand of her hair between my fingers as she unzips my fly and pulls my erect cock free.

She looks stunned for a moment, and it's as she's eyeing me with curiosity and fascination that I remember the innocence we've stolen from her. She'd never been with a man before coming into our home, and now, she's being shared by three. I might worry it is too much for her all at once, but the little vixen at my feet leans forward and nips at my shaft lightly, her playful gaze easing my fears. *She wants this as much as we do.*

Suddenly, she pulls me into her mouth, one hand wrapping around my base while the other steadies herself on my thigh. It's exquisite, the feeling of her velvet tongue caressing my cock, and I groan, marveling at the ease with which her jaw opens around me.

"Fuck, Brielle. What a good girl." I drop my head back, my hips moving in time with her mouth as she bobs, sucking and pulling, releasing and gripping, until I'm close to spilling down her throat. *I can't finish before we've gotten started.* I pull back, freeing myself from her mouth, and chuckle at the dissatisfied whimper that leaves her swollen lips.

"Everett, I wasn't—"

"Your reward will continue in a moment, pet, but first…I want you to take off your clothes." I'm panting, my cock twitching from the edge I'm still walking, but I resist the urge to shove myself back past those perfect lips. I want to ensure she continues to behave, so I'm going to give her a little…*incentive.* "Now, pet."

It takes her a moment to comply, but eventually, she pushes herself to her feet, her hazel eyes trained on me as she peels out of her clothes. It's not the first time I've seen her naked, but still, she manages to stall the breath in my lungs as if it's the first time I've seen her this gloriously *bare* and waiting for my next order. *I hope this feeling never changes.*

"Sir?" Brielle is leveling me with a calculating and curious gaze, her brow raised as she attempts to predict what I'm planning next.

"Remind me of your safewords." I wrap my arms around her waist and pull her toward me, steadying her with my hands as she looks up at me through thick lashes.

"Yellow, to warn you that I'm getting uncomfortable, and red to make everything stop." She blushes at my approving smile and tilts her head, her imagination, no doubt, running wild with possible scenarios. Unfortunately for her—luckily for me—the innocence and inexperience of her previous life will ensure that my plan is a surprise. I grin down at her and move.

"Everett!" She squeals as I lift her, maneuvering and turning her until her thighs are wrapped around my neck and her hands are pressed against my thighs. She pushes herself up, her large eyes finding me over her shoulder as her face flushes a deep crimson from the position. "T-this is—"

"Part of your reward, pet. You accepted your punishment with grace, Brielle, and you've pleased me. So now...I'm going to please *you*."

Chapter Nine

Brielle

The heat of his words brush against my center, caressing the exposed, wet flesh, and cause a whimper of anticipation to escape my parted lips. I adjust my weight, grateful for the upper body strength my schooling and training have built, and dip my chin to take him back in my mouth.

Like his face, he keeps himself shaved, and I relish in the soft feeling of his skin against my lips as I bob my head around him, pulling him deeper into my mouth as his tongue darts out to caress my folds.

"Fuck, Brielle." He curses as he tastes me, stroking and exploring the most intimate part of my body as a low growl of approval slips from the back of his throat. His fingers, tight around my waist, keep me steady as he greedily laps up my arousal, his cock hardening further as my wetness coats his tongue.

I moan, distracted by his tongue as it works me delicately, spearing my pussy as I pull him deeper into my throat, my heartbeat loud in my ears as the blood rushes to my head. I'd heard, in passing, my classmates giggling while talking about this position, but never when I'd imagined it, had I expected something like *this*.

I wrap a hand around the base of his cock and pump him as I withdraw, stopping so that only the head of his cock remains in my mouth. I caress him, tasting the salty bite of his excitement, and giggle as he groans, his hips pressing forward as he attempts to slide himself back into my mouth.

"Pet," he cajoles lightly, his tongue slow as it skims my aching and sensitive clit. I jump, the sudden spark of pleasure nearly making me lose my grip around him, my reaction only causing him to chuckle and steady me with his arm. He brings my clit into his mouth, nipping at the swollen bundle of nerves, and I cry out, convulsing around him as my earlier denied orgasm finally explodes through me.

"Fuck, Everett!" I gasp, slipping him back into my mouth, an urgent need growing within me as I continue to ride the waves of my orgasm. *I need to taste him*. I pull him deep into my throat, so deep I nearly gag, and suck, as my other hand continues to pump him, a vigorous and incessant motion that brings him back to the edge.

"I'm close, pet." He breathes the warning, attempting to give me time to retreat, but I only pick up my pace, moaning in satisfaction as his salty seed spills into my throat. "God. Fuck, Brielle."

I swallow, drinking his cum and licking his shaft so that not a drop is left behind. When I'm finished, he sighs in satisfaction and maneuvers me so that I'm back on my feet, wobbly from my release, and panting from the position.

He strokes my face, his breathing ragged as he holds me in his arms, his brown gaze sated and satisfied. "Did you enjoy that, pet?"

"Yes, sir." I smile, leaning into him as he lifts me back into his arms. He kisses my forehead and carries me toward the bed, gently laying me down and crawling in beside me.

"Good. I hope you've learned that behaving is much more pleasurable than what little satisfaction you get from breaking my rules," he chides, laughing as I nod enthusiastically.

"Much more pleasurable," I agree with a yawn, my lids already heavy with sleep. "Don't let me sleep forever this time, okay? I promised Rhys I would help with dinner."

"I'll wake you in an hour," he promises, kissing my cheek as I close my eyes and drift off to sleep.

* * * *

Everett wakes me as promised, and leaves so that I can wash up and find some new clothes. It's quick work, washing my body, selecting new underwear, and tugging on a fresh outfit, so I'm downstairs before either of the brothers have the chance to expect me.

The voices of Rhys and Everett—who are home today to rest and babysit me—travel to me from the kitchen, their lowered whispers floating past the guard hovering nearby. This guard is one of the few I've come to recognize. He's someone who, in the past week, has become a regular on our home security detail, but despite knowing his face I'm yet to have been told his name. The hired men rarely speak, and they mostly reside in the shadows, disappearing when I come into the room or, if they're unable to, acting as if I don't exist when they do catch my eye. Whether that be of their own gumption or the brothers' orders, I've yet to find out.

"I'm telling you, she's not ready." Everett's raised voice carries into the foyer, and I pause, stalling just on the other side of the wall. Are they talking about *me*?

"She deserves to know," Rhys hisses, and I peer around the corner, watching as he gestures to the tablet sitting between them. I don't mean to eavesdrop, but I can't get my feet to move either, my body cemented in place as I strain my ears, listening. "We have to tell her."

"I'm not making the call without Xander," Everett snaps, waving off the concerned look of his brother as he rolls his neck, stressed and angry.

What is going on?

"Are you snooping, Amour?" Xander's chuckle comes from behind me and makes me jump, my face flushing with heat as I'm caught red-handed. I falter, unsure of how to respond, as he levels me with those eyes, a questioning look raising his brow. "Come on. It sounds like there's something we all need to discuss."

He reaches out and takes my hand, his fingers hesitantly wrapping around my own so that he can tug me forward, exposing me from where I'd been hiding, and leading me toward the kitchen.

"Flower? What're you doing?" Rhys questions, reaching forward and shutting off the tablet lying between them.

I blink, chewing on my lower lip as I contemplate what to say. I want to ask them what they're hiding from me. I want to see what is on that tablet but…can I handle it? They certainly don't think so. I hate being excluded from a situation that revolves entirely around *me*, but I can't say that I blame them for keeping me at a distance.

I've been strained, physically and mentally, by the events of this past week, and they can see the toll it's taking on me. Every missed hour of sleep, every skipped meal, they're tracking and adding to the already long list of reasons why I *can't* help. I *want* to help. I want to understand what's happening. I want to know why this mystery man is after me.

"What did you find?" Xander nods toward the piece of technology lying between his brothers, and holds out his hand, growling in annoyance as they hesitate to pass it over.

Rhys eyes me nervously. "It's George."

"My father?" I take a step forward, attempting to see the screen as they unlock the tablet and pass it to Xander, but he turns, ensuring I'm unable to see the video as it loads on the tablet.

"Brielle, we've been trying to locate your family…" Xander pauses, allowing me a moment to swallow the shard-like truth of his words, the edge of realization cutting me as I slowly breathe it in.

Sammy. My father. They've been missing?

"It looks like we've found footage of the last place your father was seen, but —"

"Let me see it." I can't help the fear that causes me to interrupt him or the anxiety that makes my hands tremble, a wave of unease sweeping over me as I reach for the tablet.

I know I need to calm down. I know that they're watching me, assessing me, and the panic beginning to swell in my chest, but I can't help the worried thoughts that begin to spiral through my head. Is he hurt? Dead? Did he ever find Sammy, tucked away in those woods? I need answers before the unknown *drowns* me.

"Show me."

Chapter Ten

Xander

I don't regret showing her the footage. Even as the tears prick her eyes, and the breath stalls in her lungs. I needed to see this. I needed to know that she is capable of handling this world. *Our world.*

"Where is this?" Her voice is unsteady, but, given the circumstances, that's not unexpected. She swallows, and I can see her struggling to hide the emotions swelling in her throat as she rewatches the footage playing on the tablet in her grasp.

"It's a strip club downtown. Owned by The Wolves," I answer, watching as the video plays again. Her father, obviously beaten and bloodied, is being forced out the back door by a man, concealed by the shitty camera angle and a hood pulled tightly over his head. I'm certain that it's Lincoln, although the trunk of the car he shoves Beaumont into is too high above his pay grade to belong to him. Which means, there *is* someone else involved, but…*who?*

"Do you know who owns that car?" Brielle asks, passing the tablet back to Everett.

He shakes his head, and I know that he's frustrated—*pissed*—that they hadn't been able to find more in their search. *At least they found this.* At least we know that George was still alive when he'd been shoved into the trunk of this car. "They were smart enough to take the plates off and, unfortunately, it's a pretty common car up here in the city."

"Do you still think he stole that money from you?" I'm not prepared for the anger that she aims in my direction, but I can't exactly say that it's unearned. Despite the recent strides that we've made, I'll never be able to take back those first few days of her captivity, or the anger I continue battling in her presence.

I growl and drop my head, hating the quietness that's begun to seep into the room. "I don't know. I wish I had the answers, Amour, but I don't."

She seems surprised by my honesty, and her eyes soften as she looks between the three of us. Again, I can't do anything but *wish* that I had the fucking answers she's searching for.

"What do we do now?" she whispers.

Rhys rounds the island and goes to her, wrapping her in his arms and pulling her into his chest as he kisses her head and rubs her back. He's trying to soothe her, to ease the fear that's beginning to crawl up her spine, but even I can tell that his normally effective methods aren't working this time.

"We'll figure it out, Flower. I promise we're going to get to the bottom of this." Rhys smooths a hand down her hair, his green eyes darting between Everett and me as the room falls silent, again.

I know that I need to come up with a plan, and soon, if I'm going to fix this fucked-up situation I've gotten us involved with. I know I should be pissed at this whole mess, for Brielle, and my family, but I can't help the selfish piece of me that is grateful for the circumstances that brought us here. If not for Lincoln, I would have never met Brielle, and this woman is going to help me change, for the better. *I hope.*

* * * *

Lincoln

George fucking *reeks.*

I scrunch up my nose, attempting to block out the smell of his vomit, piss and *shit* as I pass by the open room where he's chained.

"P-please, w-water." His voice is nearly desolate of any sound, but I can make out the garbled plea as I tread down the hall toward my makeshift kitchen.

"You know the rules, Beaumont," I call over my shoulder, chuckling to myself at the pathetic cry that bounces off the cement walls behind me.

The warehouse we're in has been abandoned for years but still has enough power left in the generators to operate the lights and a small hot plate I use to cook up Draven's special order of poison. I'm not sure what his plan is, but honestly, the money is good enough to keep me from asking any questions. My debts are paid off, which is a blessing, and a curse. A blessing, because now I don't have to watch my back every time I walk down the streets, but a curse, because now, Draven *owns* me.

"The money's good," I hiss as I flip on the hot plate and ready the small saucepan over the coils. It's dirty, it's *all* dirty, but it's not my veins I'm injecting this shit in, so I really couldn't fucking care less. I just have to be sure I don't kill him. *That,* I know, is not part of Draven's plan.

I drop a singular crystal onto the bottom of the pot once I know it's hot enough and watch as it melts into a sticky liquid, primed for the syringe. I ready the needle, pull the liquid into the barrel, and place my thumb over the plunger before I start back down the hall to George.

His wrists are cuffed to the armrests of a wooden chair, and he's pressed back against a wall, his feet tied in front of him with rope to ensure that he's immobile enough to stay out of trouble. When he spots the needle in my hand, he shouts and writhes in his bindings, cursing and begging with what little strength he has left in him.

"P-please d-don't." He drops his head as I near him, knowing that he's vulnerable and incapable of stopping me. I brush off his pleas as I prepare his arm, pulling a piece of string around his biceps tight enough to force one of his veins to protrude from his skin. "I have ch-children, please, don't k-kill me."

"You're not going to die, George." I roll my eyes as I pierce him with the needle, my thumb pressing down slow enough to prolong the burning sensation of the drugs entering his system. He grunts and pulls at his restraints, struggling until his body succumbs to the meth beginning to burn through his bloodstream. I guess the fucker *does* need water.

The burner in my pocket buzzes, and as I fish it out, I catch a glimpse of the clock on the display. *I'm going to be late.* "I'll be back with some water for you tomorrow, George."

I kick the limp man's booted foot and stomp off to clean up, itching to get out of this building. I've never been a gambling man before, but I'd bet that whatever Draven has in store for me is much more rewarding than playing warden.

Chapter Eleven

Brielle

I'm distracted after dinner. Distraught, and damaged. I can't seem to pull my mind away from the image of my father's swollen and broken face, or the fear that was engraved on his features as he was shoved into the back of the car. How much pain had he endured that night? How much pain has he endured since? And Sammy...? What's happened to him?

"Brielle." Rhys' voice pulls me out of my spiraling thoughts, his hand soft as it caresses my own. I blink as I look up at him, forcing a smile onto my shaking lips as I attempt to pretend that their earlier discovery isn't still tearing me apart. "Flower, I think you need to blow off some steam."

"I'm not sure sex is going to help right now, Rhys." I shove at his chest, hating the smile that slips onto my face as he gasps, seemingly offended by my response.

"That's not what I was suggesting, but I like where your mind took the invitation." He winks, and wraps an arm around my shoulders, laughing as he pulls me out of the kitchen and into the living room where Everett and Xander are hunched over the tablet.

They've been studying that footage since we finished eating, discussing strategies, looking for hints as to where they might've taken my father, searching and desperate for *anything* that might be able to help us.

"Then what were you suggesting?" I smirk at him, watching him through my lashes as he pushes back his blond waves and eyes his brothers mischievously.

"I think we all need to go *out*," Rhys speaks loud enough for his brothers to hear and places enough emphasis on the last word to steal Xander's attention away from the tablet.

He growls, his head shaking back and forth as the air hisses past his clenched teeth. "Have you lost your fucking mind, Blaze? Absolutely not."

"Xander, come on, we could all use the—"

"Do I need to remind you what happened the last time she left this house?" Xander snaps, his voice so harsh that I flinch in Rhys' grasp. I can see the regret on his face as soon as the words make it past his lips, but he forces back the guilt as he stands and shakes his head. "It's not safe."

"Why can't we go outside?" I question, hating the anger radiating off Xander in waves.

"Not outside, pet, *out*," Everett corrects, locking the tablet and setting it on the coffee table.

"Out, is what we call our club, Once Upon a Time," Rhys clarifies, reading the confused expression on my face. He strokes my cheek with his thumb and eyes his brothers, raising a brow before nodding toward the front door. "We have a security detail, and all of our establishments have surveillance systems in place to cover the exits. She'll be safe."

"No, Rhys. I'm not going to risk—"

"Xander…" I'm hesitant and quiet as I interrupt him, fearing the explosive anger I've come to expect from him. "I promise I won't wander off. Please, let us go. I feel like a caged bird, trapped in these walls."

He's pacing, his hand raking through his beard as he eyes me. I can see his mind racing, contemplating his answer as he tries to reel in the anger burning through his chest.

Finally, he breathes out his response through his teeth. "Fine. I don't like it, but…go. I won't keep you caged, Amour."

He growls as he starts toward the foyer, intent on running away, but I grab his arm as he passes me to stop him. He winces at my touch but doesn't pull his arm away, stalling long enough to glance down at me over his shoulder.

"Aren't you coming?" I ask, but even as the question floats past my lips, I realize that I know the answer. *He's not coming with us.*

"Go and have fun, Amour." He shrugs out of my grasp and looks to his brothers, his icy gaze freezing me in my place. "Keep her safe, or I'll have your fucking asses on a platter."

He storms off before any of us can raise any sort of rebuttal or argument, his footsteps loud in the silent home. I sigh as I look between Everett and Rhys, worried about the repercussions going out is going to bring, but grateful for the opportunity to get out of this house. A distraction from the madness. A break.

"Well…? What should I wear?"

Chapter Twelve

Rhys

I am regretting my little shopping spree less and less.

"Beast is going to fucking kill us," Everett mutters under his breath, his brown eyes heated with lust as we watch Brielle slowly descend the stairs. She's wearing the red satin dress that I bought for her and has paired it with matching heels, the extra height provided by the shoes lengthening her legs and making the already short skirt appear even shorter. She's *beautiful*.

"Are you ready, Flower?" I grin, holding out my arm for her as she reaches the bottom step. She nods, her lip tucking between her teeth as she pushes a curly strand of hair behind her ear. She's nervous, her restless hands tugging at the edge of her dress as she attempts to force the fabric further down her legs, her flushed face only darkening once she realizes we're watching her.

"Stop fidgeting, pet. You look ravishing." Everett reaches out and gently swats at her hand, smirking as the fabric rises back up her thighs. "I'm not sure we'll be able to keep our hands off you."

She shivers at his compliments, her nipples pebbling beneath her dress as excitement swells in her veins. I lean down and nip at her exposed ear, the heat of my breath causing a small moan to leave her parted lips. "Tempting enough to want a taste."

I lick the shell of her ear before straightening, my hand pressing against her exposed lower back as I coax her toward the front door, chuckling at the confused expression that flicks across her features. It's the first time she's used the front door and, in this dress, I'm half tempted to haul her over my shoulder in commemoration of our first meeting. There'd be no way to hide in that position.

"Evening, Joe. Is everything ready?" My voice is low as I greet our head of security, Joseph, just outside the main door, his eyes downcast as he attempts to look anywhere but at our girl. *Beast's orders.*

"Yes, sir." Joe's confirmation is short and sweet as he leads us down the path toward the waiting black SUV. It's nothing fancy, but it's been decked out with enough safety measures — tinted windows, bulletproof paneling and glass — to keep Xander's broiling anger at bay. *For tonight, at least.*

I open up the backdoor for Brielle before Joe has the chance, and wave him off as she slips inside, my eyes locked on the hem of her skirt as it rises just enough to showcase the lower part of her ass cheeks. *Fuck.*

My cock starts to harden in my slacks, and I groan, my hands involuntarily reaching out to grope at the exposed flesh, her responsive gasp making me laugh as

I slip in beside her. "No bending over tonight, Flower. Our eyes are the only ones that are allowed to see this perfect ass, all right?"

Everett climbs into the car on the other side of Brielle and flings an arm over her shoulders, his brown eyes dark as he scowls at me.

"The only thing more revealing than this dress is her fucking birthday suit. You couldn't have picked anything more—"

"Sir—" Her sweet voice is soft as she interrupts him, her body turning to showcase an ample amount of cleavage as she leans toward him. "You can't be too mad at him when you're *also* enjoying the show."

Her hand floats down and lands in his lap, her small palm pressing against the budding erection growing between his legs.

"Easy, pet. Don't start something you can't finish." His warning makes her giggle, and she glances between us, daring us to make the next move. *What a devious little hellcat.*

"Having an audience won't keep you safe from us, Flower. We've never been afraid to put on a show," I murmur, my words settling into the still car as Joe opens the driver-side door. She panics, her hand quick to slide back into safer territory as he climbs behind the wheel and eyes us in the rearview mirror.

"The club has been prepared for your arrival. Three men will accompany you in, and the rest will remain with the vehicles." Joseph's voice is low and steady, his eyes turning back toward the road as he begins to maneuver us down the drive.

"Have they all been briefed on our protocol?" Everett asks, his lips curling into a smirk as Brielle looks up at him curiously.

"Yes, sir." Joseph nods.
No one touches what is ours.

* * * *

It takes thirty minutes to get downtown, and another five to reach Once Upon a Time. The parking lot is packed, but a perk of owning one of the most exclusive clubs in the city is not having to fight for a parking space. Joe drives us into a gated back section of the parking lot, and gestures for us to wait while a matching vehicle parks beside us, the windows tinted enough that an onlooker would have no idea which one we reside in. On cue, three men slip from the backseat of the car and scan the lot, checking for any possible threat before waving at us to follow them inside. The entrance, on the lower level of our multilevel building, is classic, with marble flooring, pillars, chandeliers and crisp paint. Brielle seems astonished, her hazel eyes large and wandering as she scans the room with a nervous grin, her small hands continuously — *anxiously* — smoothing over her dress. It catches my attention, and I realize as she begins worrying her lip between her teeth, that the confidence I'd once admired about this bold woman, has dwindled since the attack. *How can I fix it?*

"Don't be nervous, Flower. No one in there is going to compare to you," I whisper down to her, grabbing her hand so I can tug it away from her body. She shoots me a shy grin, a light pink tingeing her cheeks, and nods, exhaling an uncertain breath as we reach the hostess stand. It's a large counter set to partially block the row of elevators behind it, and Marie, one of our longtime workers, smiles from behind it when she spots us.

"Blaze, Brass, welcome back!" She's wearing a black sequined jumpsuit that catches the light when she moves and has her signature red curls pinned up to showcase her long neck. Her almond eyes narrow as she scans us, their green color filling with curiosity as she takes in the woman on my arm. "A newcomer, I see." She can't hide her fascination — the Grimm Brothers *never* bring guests — as she leans across the counter to get a better look at Brielle, her cat-like gaze slicing up and down the small woman at my side before a smile pulls onto those red-painted lips. "What shall we call you?"

"Rose." Everett's voice is calm and collected as he provides that damnable nickname, his brown eyes swinging to me as Brielle stiffens beside him. My mouth is open, an angry objection forming on my tongue, but he shakes his head, the tiny movement silencing me before my rant has even begun. *Not here.* I growl and tuck Brielle into my side, caressing her tense back as Marie quickly types the name Brielle will be using on this premises into our system.

"A show will begin on the third floor in twenty minutes. If you'd like to participate or book a slot for yourself, just let me or another worker know. As always, if you need a key for the fourth floor —"

"We'll call." My voice is sharp as I interrupt her, my anger evident as I glare at my brother. He waves me off, gesturing toward the bank of elevators, and I turn, leading Brielle toward them. She's silent as I press the button, those round hazel eyes scanning Everett and the three large men hovering behind us.

When the elevator doors finally open, I tug her in behind me and growl, turning on Everett as soon as the doors have closed. "What the fuck were you thinking?"

"If word travels that we're allowing *Rose* out of the house, we may be able to lure Lincoln out of hiding." Everett's brown eyes don't leave Brielle, who's still stiff and uncertain at my side.

"You're using her as fucking bait?" I can hardly contain my anger, my jaw working rhythmically as I glower at him. Xander is going to be fucking *pissed*.

"I'll do whatever it takes." I'm not prepared for Brielle's response, and from the look on Everett's face, neither was he. She offers us a small smile and shrugs, her brown curls falling delicately over her shoulders. "I *hate* standing by while you all work so tirelessly for me... I'm glad I can do something to help."

Chapter Thirteen

Brielle

Oh my *god*.

I feel my mouth fall open, my mind too distracted by the room in front of me to hear the rest of the brother's hissed conversation. I know that Everett's decision won't go unpunished—the brothers seem to rarely make decisions without consulting one another first—but despite the anger that he'll no doubt face once we get back, he seems proud of the choice that he's made. I, for one, am grateful for the opportunity.

"Are you ready?" Rhys questions, trying and failing to mask the anger still tensing his jaw. I blink, falling back into the present, and my eyes, once again, rake over the large and expansive space before me. It's *huge*.

I nod, unsure if my voice will carry above the loud music thumping through the room. *How did we not hear this downstairs?* The room is dark, giving off the illusion of privacy despite the crowded level, and is mostly consumed by the bar at its center. The dark oak wood gives the space a sophisticated and elaborate feel, elevating the room in a way that matches the first level, despite the stark contrast in styles. Rounded booths fill the vacant space, their seats made of black, rich leather, and a raised runway spans from one corner of the room to the other, the path only interrupted by the bar that rises at its center.

"What's the catwalk for?" I have to yell to be heard over the music, my curiosity earning a light laugh from Rhys and Everett.

"Patience, pet. You'll learn soon enough." Everett smiles and motions toward the bar, his brow raised as he closes the small distance between us. "Would you like something to drink?"

"Yes, sir." I nod, my stomach curling with anticipation as he leads me toward a nearby booth and gestures for me to have a seat.

I slide in, my dress so short that I can feel the smooth leather against my ass, and shift as my men move in beside me, bracketing me in the booth as our bodyguards move away to scout the room. They disappear into the shadows as the music finally softens, a lone woman appearing on the walkway on the other side of the room. *Is she...naked?*

"Ready, Flower?" Rhys chuckles. His hand drops to caress my knee, and his fingers are soft and gentle as the woman begins to saunter up the catwalk, her body twirling and swaying as she walks. It's as she gets closer to our booth that the light catches on her, and I realize that she's not *completely* naked.

"What are...those?" My gaze is locked on the small contraptions pinching her nipples, my stomach curling as my eyes follow the chain that connects the two pieces and trails down her abdomen before disappearing between her legs.

"Nipple clamps." Everett's breath hisses against my ear, the heat of his words making me shiver with desire.

"What're they for?" I never could have imagined that I'd be comfortable staring at a naked woman, and I certainly never imagined that I could be turned on by the sight of one.

"Pain. Pleasure. Both, if you use them correctly," Everett rumbles, his hand reaching beneath the table to squeeze my thigh. "Intrigued, pet?"

I nod, my mouth parting open in a surprised gasp as the woman walks up to our booth, her eyes easily finding mine across the table. "Can I get you all something to drink?"

"Whiskey, neat," Rhys and Everett reply in unison, their hands unmoving from my legs as the woman's attention turns to me.

My face flushes with heat, a tingling sensation settling between my thighs as I try to look anywhere but at the women's exposed and tortured breasts. "What do you have?"

"Oh, honey, we've got anything you could possibly desire." Her laughter is light, and her joke makes the men on either side of me chuckle as she stands, unashamed and proud, in front of us. That's what's making my mouth dry with unrequited temptation...not her body, but her *confidence*. It's astonishing.

"She'll have an amaretto sour," Rhys orders for me, and I bite my lip, my eyes still locked on the naked woman. She nods politely and shoots a wink in my direction before sauntering back across the catwalk toward the bar, the chain that had disappeared between her legs reappearing in the crack of her ass. *Oh.*

"Soak it all in, pet. Tonight is about enjoying yourself," Everett rumbles.

"Look, Flower." Rhys points his chin toward the end of the catwalk, and I look over as a man and woman make their entrance. The man is wearing a leather thong, the bulge of his erection straining against the unforgiving fabric, and the woman is wearing a latex bodysuit, her dark hair pulled back in a tight ponytail, which swings behind her back as she waves. She's holding something, and I'm not sure what it's for until her arm moves forward to snap it across the man's exposed ass. I jump.

"That's a riding crop," Everett informs me before I have the chance to ask, his hand sliding higher up my thigh while Rhys continues stroking my knee.

"Is it for punishment or pleasure?" The question is a breathy moan, my chest rising and falling as I pant needily at the sight in front of me. *This is all so…erotic.*

"Both. Right now, I'd say that man is enjoying a reward rather than enduring a punishment." Everett smirks and crouches down to hiss in my ear. "I'd like to use something like that on you."

I gasp, my hand reaching up to press against my lips as his fingers stretch toward the hem of my skirt, the exploring digits stopping just beneath the fabric so that I can almost imagine their heat against my center. *Can he tell how wet I am?* I press my thighs together, trapping his hand in an attempt to keep it from rising any further, embarrassment and excitement swirling in my stomach. I'm at war with myself. While a piece of me is worried about the possible ridicule I could face once he realizes how turned on I am by these strangers, and another is afraid of being caught with his hand between my legs, that small, naughty, and unexplored piece of me is *begging* that I let him continue. *What am I going to do?*

"Problem, Brielle?" Rhys' low laughter fills my ears as he tugs at my knee, pulling it toward him until my thighs and legs are parted once more. I groan as Everett's fingers find my sex, his tantalizing touch stroking my soaking folds as I gasp and writhe against the seat, the pleasure and fear almost too much to bear. "Try to keep your voice down, Flower. If I wanted the whole room to see my brother playing with your pussy, I'd have taken you up to the third level."

What? What the *hell* is on the third floor? The question is there, and I want to ask, but Everett's finger slides into me, erasing my thoughts and fears and replacing them with pleasure, lust and *need*. I bite my cheek, trying to muffle my moans as his finger slips in and out of me, his free hand clamped on my other knee to ensure my legs are kept open for him.

"Two whiskey neats and an amaretto sour." Our waitress has returned with a tray of drinks, her smile wide as she scans the three of us, completely unaware and oblivious of what's going on beneath the table. *Oh god.* I force a smile, because really I'm not capable of much else at the moment, and raise my hand to take the drinks from her as she begins to pass them across the table. I set Rhys' and Everett's down, but as I'm taking mine from her small hands, Everett pushes another finger into me, a mischievous grin slicing across his face. *Fuck!* I'm barely able to contain my moan, the coppery taste of blood blooming across my tongue as I tear into my cheek to keep quiet, my eyes shutting for a moment or two as I attempt to collect myself.

"Can I get you three anything else?"

Fuck, just go away!

"I think we're good for right now, thanks." Rhys nods, a knowing smirk lifting his lips as Everett continues to work me.

"Everett." I breathe out, trying to squeeze my legs closed as another woman, this one wearing a maid's uniform, bustles past with more drinks.

"Don't hide from me, Brielle." Everett's voice is rough with desire, and I succumb to the hands prying my legs apart, all too aware of the erections beginning to grow in their slacks. *I want them. I* need *them.*

I reach toward Rhys' groin, but he redirects my wandering hand to his thigh, his head nodding toward the catwalk as another woman begins to strut down it. This one is bound with red rope, the intricate ties twisting around her breasts and ribs before disappearing behind her back where her arms have been secured. An unbidden moan slips past my sealed lips.

"We may need to invest in one of those if you can't keep quiet, Flower," Rhys hisses, leaning down to nip at my ear as a man leads a collared woman past, a black ball gag resting behind her teeth.

"Do you like the theme tonight?" Everett chuckles, his thumb reaching up to press against my clit. I writhe, my hips involuntarily moving to match the pace of his thrusting fingers.

"BDSM always seems to draw a crowd." Rhys' lips trail down my neck, and I glance across the room to spot our waitress heading back in our direction. I reach out and clasp my drink, desperate to hold onto something, *anything*, as she approaches us.

"Can I get you another?" She's talking to Rhys, and when I glance down at his free hand—the one not holding me open—I can see that his glass of whiskey is already empty.

"Please." Rhys passes her the glass, and I thank god that she's about to leave, my sensitive clit aching as Everett swipes the pad of his thumb across it again. "I don't think we caught your name earlier."

Rhys! I gasp, shifting in my seat as Everett curls his fingers inside me, pressing them up into the sensitive ball of nerves within me while circling my clit tauntingly. *Fuck, fuck, fuck!* I start drinking. I down my glass of bourbon, desperate for the distraction the burn of alcohol creates as it slides down my throat, and breathe out a rough sigh as I pass the emptied glass to her.

"Could I get a refill too, please?" I manage to keep my voice level as I feel the peak of my orgasm beginning to build, my hands clasping together on the tabletop as she nods and turns back toward the bar.

"Not here, please…" I trail off as Rhys grabs onto my chin, turning my face so that I'm looking at him. His green eyes are blazing with fire, and he leans into me, devouring my lips as Everett pushes me over the edge. I come, my pussy clamping around his fingers, my moans swallowed by Rhys as our lips mash together desperately. His tongue dances with mine and I ride the waves of my orgasm, grinding against Everett's hand as Rhys steals the breath from my lungs.

I'm panting by the time I've finished, my thighs sticky with my release, and my face hot with arousal. Rhys pulls away, smiling down at me as Everett licks his fingers clean, their hands still resting on my thighs when the waitress returns. I'm silent as she passes us our replenished glasses, too embarrassed to meet her sultry gaze as I thumb the edge of my tumbler.

"You guys just flag me down if you need another refill, okay?" She laughs before turning to take care of another table, the chain around her body clinking as she moves.

"Fix your dress, pet. We're going to the third floor."

Chapter Fourteen

Everett

Brielle shifts in her seat, and I watch as her hands dip beneath the table to straighten her rumpled skirt, her pale cheeks still tinged with pink from her recent orgasm. It takes what little self-control I have left to keep my dick from growing hard again, the mere thought of her riding my hand while tonguing my brother enough to make it jolt in my pants. *If I don't get a grip now, I'll never leave this damn booth.*

She nods when she's ready, her curious eyes following Rhys as he slips from the booth, his tall, lean body angled toward the wall of elevators as he checks the watch on his wrist.

"We're just in time for the show." He smiles, winking at me as Brielle rises from her seat and grabs her drink. The leather where she'd been sitting is damp, and I groan as I toss back my whiskey, clinging to the distraction the burn of alcohol causes as it slides smoothly down my throat. I leave the emptied glass and a tip on the table before following them, my eyes scanning the dark room for the familiar faces of our guards as I reach them at the elevators.

"Is the *show* similar to this?" Brielle's voice carries easily over the music that's beginning to fill the space again, her body swaying in time with the beat as she gestures toward the waiters and waitresses bustling around the space.

"You'll see." Rhys smirks, sipping on his drink as our guards finally appear to join us. He hits the button with his elbow, his free hand snaking out to wrap around her waist as she sways, the alcohol already beginning to dampen the unease that had unsettled her.

"Come on, pet." I take her hand, turning her and leading her into the elevator as the doors open for us, the bright white light of the car illuminating the darkened level. Once the doors have shut, the music disappears, and Brielle looks up at me quizzically. "Each level is soundproof."

She nods, but her lips remain twisted in curiosity as we ride to the third floor. Stepping off is like stepping into another world, and Brielle backtracks, her eyes widening with surprise.

"Easy, Flower. We've got you." Rhys chuckles, wrapping her into his side as he leads her into the room.

People are everywhere—in chairs, on couches, in booths, or by the bar, but *no one* is on the stage at the center of the room. *That* won't be occupied until the show begins.

Brielle takes a sip of her drink and swirls the remaining liquid, her eyes tentative as she scans the crowd. "I hadn't realized there'd be so many people."

"Once Upon a Time draws a large crowd, pet. We offer a safe haven for people to explore their desires, and we cater to those needs." I shrug, grateful for the freedom this club had once provided *me*. After meeting Xander, it didn't take too long for me to realize that I needed to find a better...*outlet*...for my inner demons. These people and the walls of this building were just what I'd been looking for.

"Ladies and gentlemen, please find your seats." A female voice comes over the speakers, and Brielle straightens, looking between Rhys and me as the people at the bar begin to disperse. I take her by the waist and lead her to a nearby couch, tugging her into my lap as the voice continues. "As a reminder, the scenario you are about to see will be performed by consenting adults. Safe words have been agreed upon and are available to them if needed. Please enjoy."

Brielle shifts, unknowingly rolling her ass against my cock as she downs the rest of her liquor, her lip tucked between her teeth as her anticipation swells. *She's excited.* I chuckle and lean forward, nipping at her ear as Rhys flags down a passing waitress, ordering another drink for our girl as two workers appear on the stage. They're carrying a tantric chaise between them, and as they settle it in the middle of the bare space, Brielle glances over her shoulder at me, a silent question in her eyes that I'm unwilling to answer.

"You'll have to wait and see, pet," I murmur, tucking her closer to my chest as the waitress returns with her refilled glass. Normally, I wouldn't want her drinking this much alcohol but, she deserves a break from her inhibitions, at least for tonight.

"Are *we* going to go up there?" she asks, leaning toward Rhys as he drapes an arm over the back of the couch.

"Would you like to, Flower?" He smirks at her, his tongue slow to drag along his bottom lip as she pulls a drink from her glass.

"Not today, Rhys. She'll have had enough firsts without adding exhibitionism to the list," I cajole, earning a light laugh from him as he shrugs innocently.

"Her wish is my demand and, who knows? Our girl might just enjoy herself." He runs his thumb along her bottom lip and a small moan escapes her, the sound of her quickening breaths causing my cock to harden in my slacks as she squirms. *This woman…*

The lights flicker once before they begin to dim, silencing the crowd as a few spotlights focus on the empty stage. I can see the curiosity that glistens in Brielle's eyes, and it's as I'm admiring her full lips and the sensual curve of her body, that a small woman walks onto the stage.

"*Oh.*" Brielle's face reddens with heat, and I smirk, stroking a hand down her side as she leans forward to get a better look. The woman's wrists are bound by leather cuffs, and the two men that appear behind her are each wielding a length of chain, their cocks already erect and straining for their woman's attention.

"Do you like what you see, Flower?" Rhys' voice is low as the woman on stage turns for the crowd, displaying her body as cheers and whistles begin to filter through the large room.

Brielle nods, her eyes still focused on the stage as the woman is led toward the chaise by the two men. They bend her over the back of the chair and position her to their liking, facing her ass toward the crowd before they begin to secure her with the chains they carried on stage. One end connects to the leather cuffs around her wrists, and with practiced ease, they secure the opposite ends to hooks embedded into the floor on either side of the chaise. Locked in her position, the woman wiggles with excitement as one of the men steps up behind her and smacks her ass, the sound of her pleasure reverberating through the room loud enough to be heard over the murmurs beginning to fill the space.

Brielle's breath catches in her throat, and she chews on her lip as the man's hand runs up the woman's back, stroking her skin before he winds his fist through her hair. He tugs, pulling her head back until her chin is lifted for the other man, who has gracefully positioned himself by her mouth, his cock pressed forward and waiting for her to open her mouth. Brielle shifts in my lap, and I can almost *feel* the heat of her excitement against my leg. Fuck, am I glad she's not wearing any underwear.

"What're you thinking about right now, pet?" I chuckle into her ear and drag a hand up her thigh, brushing my fingers against her smooth skin as she shivers needily in my lap.

"Being shared by my men." She grinds against my hardening cock and leans back into my chest, her legs parting slightly as the woman begins to get fucked on stage.

"Fuck. You're insatiable, Flower." Rhys groans, his head dropping back as Brielle reaches over to tug her hand through his loose hair.

I can see her need building and her fears evaporating with each sip of liquor that touches her tongue. I want to keep her here, where she has the freedom and the confidence to explore, but my phone buzzes in my pocket reminding me of the real reason we're here. Distraction. Her worries are forgotten for the night, and Xander is ready for us to bring her home.

He's ready for her surprise.

I smirk and lace my fingers through hers. He may have been against us taking her out in the beginning, but once he realized he'd have a moment alone to prepare...he managed to swallow his anger. He's making an effort. An effort we can only hope is received.

Please, please let this work.

Chapter Fifteen

Brielle

I *may* have had too much to drink.

I sway in my seat, humming a random tune while my skin buzzes with warmth, my entire body tingling and fuzzy from the alcohol burning through my system. I'm elated. Uninhibited. Free. Of course, that's only until I remember the reason we had to leave.

"Did he say what he wanted?" My eyes dart between Everett and Rhys, who're sitting on either side of me in the backseat, the small movement enough in my drunken state to make my head spin.

Everett shrugs, feigning an ignorance that his crooked smile disproves, his brown eyes tracking me as he passes me another water bottle. He knows something, but for some reason, he's unwilling to tell me what that *something* is.

"Next time, I'm counting your drinks." He uncaps the bottle for me and pours in a small packet of dried powder, some 'cure' to the alcohol dampening my senses.

"I can handle a little alcohol," I mutter, taking a tentative sip from the bottle. I knew what I was signing up for when I finished that last glass. If I didn't *want* to be tipsy and drunk, I wouldn't have asked for another refill. *Why can't I enjoy this?*

"We just have to be careful, Flower. Xander will be pissed if he finds out how much we let you have." Rhys murmurs the explanation, attempting to make me feel better, but instead of soothing me, his words only add fire to my building flame. *Xander.* The very man who, up until I'd started enjoying myself tonight, hadn't wanted to share more than a few awkward minutes of conversation with me.

"Well, maybe *I'll* just have to get pissed about him cutting our night short," I quip, crossing my arms over my chest. I know I'm being dramatic, even as Rhys strokes my knee comfortingly, but I can't help the alcohol-fueled anger burning through me. The show had just started when Everett got a text from his brother, demanding that we come home so that he and I could finally talk. I hope he's ready. It may be the alcohol talking, but I'm going to confront him for avoiding me. I am going to get some damn answers.

* * * *

My liquid courage is waning by the time we pull up to the house. Rhys and Everett are unusually quiet beside me, unwilling to test my temper as the car slows to a stop and our guard slips out. They eye each other over my head for a beat, sharing a silent conversation I'm not privy to before Rhys nods and they both push open their doors. I half expect Xander to be waiting for us, so when we get inside and I realize that he's not pacing the floor anxious for our return, I feel a twinge of hurt beginning to intermix with my anger. Neither of which pairs well with the alcohol.

"Go check in his study, pet." Everett guides me toward the staircase with the press of his hand to my exposed lower back, his brown eyes lingering on my body for a beat too long. I feel my face flush at the attention, my stomach flipping excitedly as the desire I'd tried to squander away attempts to resurface. I brush it off, stomp it out, and force it back once again, determined to stay focused. *Answers.* I'm finally going to get my answers.

"We'll be down here if you need us," Rhys calls after me as I climb the stairs, the warmth and promise in his words melting some of the tension that's beginning to tense my spine. If Xander wounds me in battle, at least I'll have them to piece me back together.

I sigh as I turn down the hall, the alcohol still lingering in my system causing me to sway in my heels as I go. I don't knock when I reach the closed door of his study. I simply grab the handle, turn the knob, and walk inside.

"Wow…" I can't help the audible gasp that announces my entrance to the room, my mouth falling open as I turn to take in the space. I can't say that I've spent much of any time picturing what this room might have looked like, but even if I had, I don't think I would've pictured something quite like this. There are books everywhere. Wooden bookcases line the walls and wrap around the room, their frames stretching from the hardwood floor up to the vaulted ceiling. Books line each shelf, organized and pristine, with glossy edges or leather spines. There are so many, new and old, that the air smells like their pages, that light, familiar scent making tears prick my eyes as memories of my mother momentarily flit across my mind. It's astonishing. It's overwhelming. It's *amazing,* and I'm choking on a surprised fit of laughter as I spin to take in the room again. Out of all three of my men, I wouldn't have pictured a room like *this* to be Xander's haven but, sitting in the center of it all, behind a large wooden desk, he waits, watching me with a hesitant smile.

"Hello, Amour." His voice is lighter than I expect it to be, his words floating across the room as his eyes blaze a trail of heat over my body. I can almost feel him caressing me with his gaze, his fingers racing down the length of his beard as his tongue darts out to wet his lips. "Which one of my brothers do I have to thank for putting you in that dress?"

"Neither. I picked it out myself." My reply is quick, and I level with him my gaze as he stands to round his desk, his large frame almost dwarfing the table.

"*Tentatrice alléchante.* My poor brothers." He chuckles, the foreign words rolling off his tongue so naturally, I can't help but wonder how long he's known the language.

"Did you learn that from these?" I gesture around the room, lifting my chin as his eyes roam over my body again, a silent challenge to his control. He notices and swallows back a groan as he shakes his head, those icy blue orbs tracking me as I cross toward one of the shelves. I lift a book, something older, with worn leather and faded pages, and scan the cover, attempting to decipher the words scrawled across the cover.

"My mother was an immigrant from France." The smile that had been pulling up his lips has faded slightly, the light glimmering in his gaze darkening as he settles himself onto the corner of his desk. "But I didn't call you in here to talk to you about my mother."

"Why did you call me in here, then?" I snap the book closed and replace it on the shelf, careful not to disturb the order in which they are placed before turning back to face him. "Why do you want to talk to me *now*, after you've been trying so hard to avoid me?"

My words sting, a blow to his inflated ego I'm sure he wasn't expecting. I want to take them back as soon as I've said them, the reasonable side of me understanding the pain that undoubtedly causes his brashness, but I don't apologize for my boldness. He needs to understand that his insecurities and fears can be damaging to his relationships if he's not careful. He needs to understand that his actions have consequences.

"I know that we started on the wrong foot, and I know that I'm responsible for that, Brielle. I can't begin to explain the fucked-up mess that goes on in my head." He visibly deflates, his strong shoulders tilting inward as he attempts to form his thoughts into a coherent and understandable explanation. "I want to explain away the damage I know my actions have caused but, your anger is valid. I've been behaving like a fucking child, Brielle, and you deserve better."

I try not to let his words sway me, or melt the anger I'd felt before stepping into this room, but it's not working. As hurt, angry and confused as I was after he disappeared, I *understand*. I can see that he's trying. *Changing*. He just needs more time, and I'm going to have to decide how long I'm willing to give him.

"You killed that man. You had sex with me and then you avoided me for *three* days, Xander. I felt like some trashy one-night stand who you were embarrassed to have to see again." I don't know why I keep digging. Yes, I want him to understand what he's put me through, but I'm worried that a larger part of it is that I want him to feel as shitty as I've felt the past couple of days. *Does that make me a bad person?*

"I've never been good with my words, Brielle. I wasn't taught to express my emotions, I was taught to act. I want to be a better man, for my brothers, for my business, and for *you*..." He trails off, his brows furrowing together and his forehead wrinkling in discomfort. He pushes himself away from his desk and slowly crosses the room to me, his movements calculated and hesitant as he reaches a hand toward me. "I'm not *good*, Brielle. I'm a monster. A B*east*. I don't expect you to believe that I'm capable of changing—I certainly don't—but if you're willing to give me a chance, I would like to show you something."

His hand hovers in front of me, waiting for my decision. Will I trust him? Or will I punish him for the past he's trying so hard to overcome?

The answer is simple.

I take his hand.

Chapter Sixteen

Xander

Her hand is warm in mine. Every time I start to believe that I'm finally figuring her out, she catches me off guard and surprises me again. I'm never surprised, but this *woman*. She believes in me. She's going to give me the chance to show her that I can be a better man, a different man, than the one my father's hate created. I can do this...*right*?

She's silent as she walks beside me, her hazel eyes clouded with superstition and uncertainty as I lead her down the hallway toward my room. I want to explain my plan to her but I really am *no good* at explaining what I'm thinking. What I want. What I need. *I just have to show her.* I pull her to a stop in front of my closed bedroom door and release her hand, my fingers gentle as I trace them up her arm. *I can't fuck this up.*

"Close your eyes."

She cocks a brow at my whispered order, her lips pursing as she contemplates my request. I'm not sure if she's going to do as I've asked, but after a few never-ending seconds, she slowly moves her lids to comply. They flutter shut, a silent testament to her trust, that stalls me. I *really* can't fuck this up. I open the door, a lump of nerves forming in my throat as I gently tug her inside and lead her toward the center of the room. When I have her positioned where I need her, I release her again, my long legs carrying me back a few steps as I struggle to clear my throat. "Whenever you're ready, Amour."

This time, there is no hesitation. Her hazel eyes open, the swirling brown and gold color lit up by the candle flames that dance throughout the room. She gasps as she takes in the decorations, one hand lifting to cover her parted lips as she stares at the room in awe. "Xander…"

I watch her as she begins to explore the room, her fingers gracing over the strings of the balloons that press against the ceiling and her feet delicate as she steps through the rose petals that cover the floor. Candles are placed periodically throughout the space, their flames casting a romantic glow across the walls, and a large bouquet is strewn across the head of the bed. The decorations, paired with the soft music playing through my speakers, creates an elaborate, dramatic, and cheesy gesture that she deserved that night I stole that innocent piece of her.

"I didn't earn the piece of you that I took, Brielle. You shouldn't have lost your virginity like that…being *fucked* and shared by two men. If you'll let me, I would really like to make it up to you, Amour." I close the distance between us, lifting my hand to delicately brush across her cheek, and the bruise still darkening the skin beneath her makeup. Her breath is coming in small pants now, fanning past her lips and ruffling the hair that's settled around her face as she shifts, her lip tucking between her teeth.

"You did all of this for me?" She leans into my touch, the stress that had tensed her body dissipating as she watches me through thick lashes. "I know you don't believe it, Xander, but you *are* a good man. You try to hide behind your temper but... I see you."

Her words make my chest tighten, my breath stalling in my lungs as she flashes a hesitant smile up at me. She reaches toward me and, although I can anticipate her touch, I can't stop the involuntary flinch that curls my shoulders inward. She strokes my chest, her fingers wrapping into the fabric of my shirt as she tugs me toward her, her eyelids fluttering shut. I kiss her and snake an arm around her waist, pulling her against me as she melts. My heart hammers in my ears, but despite the adrenaline coursing through me, I relax, having her in my arms.

She's sweet, her lips moving delicately against my own, and I have to resist the urge to devour her as she moans into my mouth. I have to be gentle tonight. Slow. Loving. It's the least I can do after all the damage I've caused.

She opens her mouth, allowing us the opportunity to explore one another as her hips press forward, grinding against my crotch enough to cause my cock to grow hard in my slacks. I groan, dragging my tongue along hers as the kiss deepens, the sweet taste of alcohol on her breath making my head buzz with excitement.

"Xander." Her breathy sigh fills my ears, and I nip at her lip, stepping forward with her until she's backed up against the bed. She reaches for my buckle, wanting to undo my pants, but I gently direct her hand back to her side and pull away, my forehead pressed against hers.

"Lie down, Amour." My voice is a low growl that makes her shiver, her nipples pebbling beneath the thin material of her dress as she sits and settles back against the mattress. "I'm going to worship every inch of your body."

I stoop down, pressing a quick kiss to her lips before I sink down her body, my hands racing over her hips, parted thighs and calves. I hook my fingers around the clasps at her ankles, and I make quick work of the buckle, allowing her shoes to drop to the floor as I nip my way down her legs. The scent of her arousal is heady enough to perfume the air, and I groan again as I kneel by her feet.

"Xander?"

I don't answer her silent question, and instead take the opportunity her confusion provides to press a kiss to the sole of her right foot. She squirms, a small gasp rushing past her lips as I nip at her ankle and repeat the same process on her left foot. I kiss my way back up her legs, stroking, licking and nibbling on her skin, until I reach her parted thighs, and catch a glimpse of her bare pussy beneath the dress. *Fuck.*

"What a dirty girl, going out without any underwear," I muse, chuckling at the low mewl that squeals past her parted lips. *Degradation kink?* I'll have to tuck that information away for later.

I bite her thigh and lick away the sting as she squirms, her fingers twining through my hair in an attempt to pull me higher up her body, toward her aching center. I want to drag this out and tease her a little more, but tonight is about *her* pleasure, and I aim to please. I crawl up her body, pushing her dress up and dragging my hands across her exposed skin as she writhes, her anticipation building. I hover above her, blowing a warm rush of air against her swollen clit, and she jumps, aching, panting and *wet*.

"Xander, please." She whines, tugging at my curls, her hips lifting off the bed to try to urge me toward the place where she needs me most. This woman makes me fucking *weak*, and who am I to resist her?

I drag my tongue up her wet slit, growling in pleasure as the sweet and salty taste of her explodes across my tastebuds. She groans, her hips rolling in pleasure as I drag my tongue up her center to circle her clit, finally delivering pleasure where she needs it most. She moans and grips my hair, desperate for an anchor in the sea of sensations beginning to crash over her as I devour her.

"*Délicieux, mon amour.*" I breathe out a heady sigh and wrap my hands around her hips, tugging her into me as my cock grows painfully hard in my slacks. I want her so fucking bad but, I have to be patient. Tonight is about *her*.

She mewls, her head dropping back against the covers as I close my lips around her clit and pull, sucking on the sensitive bundle of nerves until her thighs are shaking against my shoulders. She comes apart around me, a loud moan of pleasure ripping from her throat as she orgasms, a rush of her sweet arousal coating my lips. I growl, a possessive, throaty sound, and lap up the liquid, caressing her until she's a shaking mess beneath me.

"Fuck, Xander, *please*." Her hands slip through my hair, her body dropping limp and sated back against the bed as I finally release her hips. She's watching me over the curves of her body, her eyes shadowed by pleasure as I crawl up her, my hardened cock pressing against her leg.

"Use your words, Amour. What do you need?"

She flushes at my question, her heavy breaths dancing across my cheeks as I begin kissing down her jaw and neck.

"I need *you*, Xander. Please. Make love to me."

What kind of man, monster or not, could resist a request like that?

Chapter Seventeen

Brielle

The hard edges of the Beast's outer walls are crumbling, so, so slowly. He's grinning down at me, a soft, warm smile, as his hand caresses my cheek, those blue eyes heavy with desire as he watches me. He may not want or be able to see it yet, but he is coming undone. *I* am undoing the Beast.

"I've never made love to anyone, Amour. I'm not sure that I've ever *loved* before but, I am willing to try…for you." His soft words make my heart skip a beat, the breath catching in my lungs as he lifts himself off me enough to remove his pants. I wait, watching in amazement as the muscles beneath his tattoo-covered skin flex and bunch in response to his movements. I want to *feel* those muscles pressed against me. I want to feel all of him.

He settles back onto me, naked from the waist down, and I raise a brow, reaching toward his shirt. "You're forgetting something."

He grimaces, wincing away from my wandering hands for a moment before he can catch himself. He breathes out, a long, hard breath, and shakes his head.

"I don't want to ruin this with my —" He pauses, his lips pressing together as he attempts to find the right word. "Disfigurations."

"Disfigurations?" The word feels dirty in my mouth, and I frown, tugging at the first button of his shirt. "You're *alive* despite these wounds, Xander. You need to embrace it."

My words make his jaw tense, a fleeting moment of weakness flickering in his gaze before he has the chance to shove it away. He nods, and rips open the shirt, tugging it off his shoulders and down his corded arms until the ruined fabric falls off the side of the bed.

"Only for you, Amour." He almost chokes on the words as I run my fingers over the scars littering his chest. With the tattoos covering his skin, I hadn't realized the sheer number of injuries he's sustained. His entire torso is scattered with puckered skin and indented flesh from where he's been gouged or stabbed. What kind of monster could do this to his child? *What hell has my Beast endured?*

I lean forward and press a kiss to one of the larger scars, surprising Xander—and myself—as my lips delicately meet his rough skin. I want to kiss away the fear and hurt he still feels from these wounds, to erase the horrible past that still haunts him. I want to heal him. I want to *help*. I skate my lips across his chest, covering and worshiping his body in the same way he had mine, touching each wound in the hopes that he'll realize that he's not defaced. He's beautiful, and he's *mine*.

I stretch up and press my lips to his, soft and gentle, a promise that despite his past, despite his scars, and despite his anger, I'm still here. His lips move harder against mine, desperate and fast as he growls out an almost feral sound of need. I spread my legs, allowing him to settle between my thighs, and I moan as the head of his cock teases me. I'm still overflowing with desire, despite my recent orgasm. I lift my hips, trying to urge him forward, but he chuckles and wraps his hand around his shaft, his eyebrows raised as his hazy blue orbs scan me.

"You want this, hmm?" he asks, his gravelly voice causing goosebumps to form along my skin. I whimper as he pumps himself slowly, longingly, and I nod up at him. "What a dirty girl, asking for my cock."

He chuckles and drags his head across my slit, wetting the head of his dick with the arousal coating my folds. The friction makes me moan, my body writhing in anticipation and need as he lines himself up with my center. *Fucking hell.* I breathe out a rush of air, my stomach so tight with need I feel as if I could come out of my skin.

"Xander." My moan is warped with the need blossoming in my chest, a breathy plea that seems to crack him. He pushes forward, and I nearly come apart at the seams. "Fuck!"

He's grinning as he fills me, his cock stretching my pussy around him until he's sheathed to the hilt, the length and size of him filling me so completely, it's almost too much for me to handle.

"Such a good girl," he murmurs, his words causing a bolt of electricity to run straight to my core, tightening my walls around him until he's quivering inside me, his teeth bared as he attempts to keep his composure. "Fucking hell, Amour."

He waits, holding himself deep until we've both adjusted to the feeling of one another before he begins to move, picking up a slow and torturous rhythm. I moan, my eyes rolling to the back of my head as he slides himself in and out of me, his cock so hard it almost hurts. *I'm going to be sore tomorrow.* I reach up and trace a hand through his trapped curls, tugging at the tie restraining them behind his neck, and pulling until they're spilling down around his shoulders toward me. A sharp breath rushes through his teeth, and he groans as I tug on his curls, using them to anchor him to me as he continues driving himself into me. It's softer than our first time. Gentler. His icy blue eyes are warmer than I've ever seen them, and they never once leave mine as he pushes me closer and closer to the edge. He delivers on his promise. He makes love to me until we're both bordering our release.

"Harder, please. I'm so close," I pant out, my hand sliding along his chest, now slick with a sheen of sweat. He smirks, a delicious growl rumbling from the back of his throat as he begins to pick up the pace, pushing into me harder and faster, until I'm falling apart beneath him. My orgasm rolls through me, the strength of it causing my pussy to clamp around his cock, squeezing and milking him until he's ready to jump over the cliff with me. He pulls out, finishing over my stomach with a heated groan, and I nearly come again, the look on his face enough to coil desire back through my stomach.

"Fuck, Brielle... You're so perfect," he murmurs, collapsing beside me and tugging me into his side. I curl around him, dropping my head onto his chest so that I can feel his heartbeat against my flushed cheek, and sigh as he runs his fingers through my waves. "Can you do something for me, Amour?"

I glance up at him through hooded eyes, the exhaustion I'd been fighting off tonight advancing on me. "Anything."

"Don't give up on me. Not yet."

I almost think in my haze that I've misheard him. I blink heavily, nodding through the fog as his gentle caresses begin to make me slip. "Never, Xander. Never."

Chapter Eighteen

Everett

"What's the plan?" Rhys shifts in the seat beside me, adjusting the gun tucked into the waistband of his jeans as he waits for a response. It's the second time he's asked, but this time, I can see that he's not going to take my silence as an acceptable reply. "You *do* have a plan, don't you?"

"I didn't ask you to come with me," I snap, huffing out an annoyed breath as I tap my fingers relentlessly against the steering wheel. I'm watching the entrance of the building in front of us, the neon signs in the window promoting a never-ending happy hour and exhilarating shows meant to get even the drunkest man's blood pumping. I roll my eyes.

"Right...so you'd have preferred that I let you go in there on your own?" He's smirking, that devious smile that always ends with *me* getting into trouble. "Without a plan?"

"We need more information." I know it's not enough. I know that I was dumb to come here without reinforcements—or a fucking *plan* in place—but...I need to get answers. *She's counting on us.*

"And you think they're going to give us the answers we're looking for?" He laughs as if the mere thought of anyone within The Wolves complying with us is hilarious.

"I wasn't going to give them a choice."

His laughter stops, and I know that my reply isn't one he was expecting to hear coming from me. He nods, a short and simple reply, before he pushes open the car door. "Let's go get some answers, then."

Getting inside is easier than I anticipated.

There aren't any bouncers at the door, and no armed gunmen are waiting inside, having anticipated our arrival at their *quaint* establishment. Truthfully, the place is disgusting. Filled ashtrays and forgotten drinks crowd the dusty tables, and the soles of our shoes stick to the floor as we enter, announcing our arrival. Despite the strangers entering their space, the men that linger around the stage and bar don't eye us for long, their attention drawn away by the booze or breasts shoved beneath their noses. The women, flicking their hair and hips on stage, or straddling the unobstructed lap in the audience, are older or tracked with enough needle marks to indicate that their sobriety is questionable or even non-existent. I'd roll over in my grave before letting Once Upon a Time look like *this*.

I lean against the bar, opposite the man working, and smirk at him as I drop my hand against the countertop, my brass knuckles thumping against the sealed wood. If *that* isn't enough to get someone's attention, I'm sure a fucking bullet will.

"Fuck me." I hear the bartender hiss under his breath, his beer gut sucking in as he straightens in an attempt to look bigger. "Roy. Take the girls to the back, will ya?"

A teenager, probably no older than sixteen, comes around the corner, an apron over his clothes and a mop in his hand. He eyes the three of us cautiously before moving to follow orders, rounding up the girls and leaving a few annoyed patrons in his wake. With the stage empty and the girls gone, the attention is quick to turn on us, their drunken eyes furrowed by anger and clouded with confusion as they stand to get a closer look.

"Brass. Blaze. What're two of the Grimm Brothers doing here, on our turf?" The bartender is leaning back against the sink behind him, his chin lifted high as he scans the others in the bar. No one here is going to be much of any help to him, and as his eyes settle back on me, widened with adrenaline, I know he's already aware of his defeat.

"We're looking for someone," I state, side-eyeing one of the men who is slowly inching his way toward the bar.

"A man who rents out one of the back rooms from you," Rhys adds, a lighter flickering in his hands. *Blaze is here to play.*

"Sorry to burst your bubble, boys, but money doesn't talk." The bartender grins, and the man who'd been sneaking up behind us lunges toward me.

I swing my fist faster than his drunken body will allow him to move, the sound of his jaw crunching beneath the brass knuckles silences the idle chatter in the room. The men are all stiff, watching as their comrade crumples without a whisper of complaint. *That'll hurt in the morning.*

I turn back to the bartender, chuckling as I make my way toward the small partition meant to keep patrons out from behind the counter. "Hey, Blaze. Do you know if broken bones talk?"

"You know what? I'm pretty fucking sure they do." Rhys nods, flattening his hands against the countertop as I round the back of the bar. The bartender is cursing, his panicked eyes flicking to the other men as he backs himself up as far as the small space will allow.

"All right, all right, who do you want?" He's holding up his hands now, surrendering before the fun has even begun.

"The fucker working with Lincoln Fisher."

* * * *

"That was fucking pointless." It's all I can do not to shout as I slam the car door closed behind me and round the front of the car, my shoulders tense as Rhys chuckles from behind me.

"It wasn't *completely* pointless." He's laughing to himself, stepping up behind me as I angrily shove open the garage door and barge into the house, the loud clanking of the door against the wall echoing through the early morning. "Can you put some pressure on that thing, please? Mrs. Claebourne is going to quit if she has to clean up any more blood."

I glance down at the bloodied opening on my lower arm, a gash from a broken beer bottle I'd been struck with during the fight.

"I'm fine. I'll see if Brielle can—"

"She's sleeping," Xander barks from the top of the stairs, his arms crossed and his face set with an all too familiar scowl as he scans Rhys and me. "What the fuck did you two do?"

"Xander...? What's wrong?" Brielle's voice is heavy with sleep, her small question floating to us from down the hall. Xander tenses, his eyes softening momentarily as he glances back toward her.

"It's nothing, Amour. You should go back to bed." His reply, of course, isn't enough to satiate our curious woman. I can hear her feet padding across the carpet, and then she appears beside him, hair mussed, eyes hooded, and body bare, aside from a T-shirt that barely scrapes her thighs.

"Rhys? Everett, what's—" A gasp swallows the rest of her question, her eyes locked on the blood beginning to trickle down my fingers. She races down the stairs, all exhaustion forgotten as she grabs my arm to inspect it. "There's glass in this." She glares up at Xander, who is still hovering at the top of the stairs. "This is nothing?" she snaps at him, shaking her head as she looks back down at the wound, her eyebrows knit together on her forehead. "I need the first aid kit. This has to be cleaned out."

"Let's go into the dining room. There's better lighting in there," I murmur, keeping my eyes low as I attempt to avoid Xander's angry gaze.

Sitting across from him at the table, I'm not sure how to justify our little mission with no new information to provide. I growl out in frustration. "They rent out the back office to whoever has the money to pay for it. No questions, no documentation, and no names."

"Who?" Brielle is attempting to jump into our conversation, her hands busy as she sorts through the first aid kit.

"So, after all of this, you still didn't find anything?" Xander barks, his hands clenched into fists on the table.

"We confirmed that Lincoln isn't working alone." It doesn't matter how gently I say his name, the mere mention of the man behind the attack in the clearing is enough to stall Brielle in her seat.

"Maybe we should finish up this conversation later." Rhys' voice is tight with concern as he reaches over to stroke a hand down Brielle's arm. It's enough to break her out of her thoughts, and she returns to pulling handfuls of items out of the kit.

"No. I'm fine." She shakes her head, opening up an alcohol swab as she shoots a look toward Xander from across the table. "Please, let me stay."

"If I think it's getting to be too much for you, I'm moving this conversation to my study, understand?" He's waiting, a silent test to see how much she can truly handle.

"Yes, I get it." She turns her attention back to my arm and nods, gripping a pair of tweezers in her hand as she begins cleaning the glass out of my wound. "Keep going."

Chapter Nineteen

Brielle

"They couldn't give us a name." Everett's voice is steady as I pull the glass from his arm, his eyes moving between Xander and me as he continues. "The room was reserved through Lincoln, but another man provided the cash for it."

I'm trying to keep my nerves at bay, but this conversation is beginning to make my heart race with adrenaline. *Keep calm, Brielle.* I can't let them shut me out of this. I have to do this for my family.

"Were they able to give you a description?" Xander's jaw is tight as he attempts to calm the anger broiling through his veins. He wants to pass the reins, to allow his brothers to ease some of the stress constantly weighing down his shoulders, but it's going to take some time. *Time I might not have.*

"White, older, and clean," Rhys mutters, scratching a hand across his trimmed beard.

I try not to linger on the first-degree burns that redden his palms or the welted handprint that's collared around his neck. I can't stomach the thought of the fight they endured. Not right now.

"Not anything we can use to go off of and, of course, they don't have any cameras set up out front or inside."

I sigh as I begin wiping down Everett's arm, thankful for the distraction and that his wound isn't large enough to require Rhys' untrained stitching skills.

"He's not someone they see around very often. They couldn't even tell us what he uses the room for." I can hear the disappointment darkening Everett's voice as he caresses my chin. I look up at him through my lashes, letting out a small breath as I lean into his touch. "I'm sorry, pet."

I swallow, my face heating as three pairs of eyes fall on me. "I just can't stand all of the fighting."

"This is our life, Flower." Rhys caresses my knee, but his words do little to comfort me.

"You're going to get yourselves killed because of me." I can't hide the panic that laces my voice as I look between my men, uncertainty making my stomach churn. "Why can't our lives just be normal?"

"Normal?" Xander laughs, an unexpected, full-belly laugh that catches us all off guard. I jump at the sound, surprised by the unfamiliar noise spilling from the darkest of the three Grimm Brothers.

"Our lives have never, and will never be normal, pet." Everett shakes his head, those brown eyes swirling with concern as he attempts to understand me, and the small world that I've come from.

"We don't know normal," Rhys confirms, his voice gentle as he continues to stroke my knee.

Xander has calmed across from me, his blue eyes scanning me, analyzing me, as we watch each other hesitantly from other worlds. "We can try, Amour, but, you'll have to show us how."

How can I possibly show them what normal life is supposed to be like, when I myself haven't felt normal in a long time? I need to figure out when I'd last felt like my world wasn't constantly tipped on its axis, but how? When did I last feel *normal?*

* * * *

I swallow as I lower myself onto the dusty carpet, my throat tight as I watch my men glance around the empty space.

"You...grew up here?" Rhys is quiet as he sits down beside me, his green, curious eyes locked on me as he tries to put himself in my place.

I nod. I'd never anticipated the emotions coming back here would unravel. I never imagined I'd set foot in this house again, let alone with three men who seem so intent on turning my world upside down. "It wasn't so run down back then."

"Which one was your room?" Xander is looking down the hall toward the vacant bedrooms, his arms crossed over his large chest as he leans against the wall.

"First one on the right." I point, attempting to swallow around the lump that's beginning to form in my throat as I gesture toward the other closed doors. "Sammy's room is next to mine, and my parent's room—" I pause, swallowing hard. "Is on the end."

"May I?" Xander jabs a thumb over his shoulder in the direction of the hall, and I nod, assuming the on-edge man wants to scope out the home.

"What was it like? Living here?" Everett asks, peeking through another doorway and into the small kitchen. It's outdated—it was always two decades behind the modern style—but it holds good memories. Memories of my mother, and my childhood before her devastating diagnosis.

"Warm." I smile, a small laugh leaving my parted lips as I lean against Rhys, his arm gentle as it wraps me into his side.

"Why has it just been sitting vacant?" I'm not sure if Rhys is looking for an answer, or simply thinking out loud, but I shrug and answer nonetheless.

"We had to file bankruptcy after all of my mother's medical bills finally drained the last of our savings. My father couldn't afford the mortgage, so the bank evicted us after we defaulted on payments... I guess they weren't able to resell it." Honestly, even as I provide the answer, I'm not sure if I truly know the real reason behind it remaining empty for all these years.

"When *we* defaulted on payments?" Everett's voice is soft as he emphasizes my words, forcing my attention to snag on another problem I struggle to face. "You were just a child, Brielle."

I shake my head in disagreement but don't push the subject any further. *I won't win.* Yes, I'd been young, but I do believe, despite raising Samuel and going to school full-time, that I should have been able to do more. They'll try to convince me otherwise but the guilt isn't something I can talk myself out of. *Not yet.*

"You're not the only one in this house that feels responsible for things that were out of their control, Flower. We've all got our inner demons," Rhys murmurs, his thumb soft as he begins to move it in small circles at my hip.

"I feel like such an open book compared to you three," I whisper, offering a hesitant smile at Xander, who's reappeared from the darkened hall, "I want every piece of each of you. Good and bad."

"All you have to do is ask, pet." Everett's voice is low as he shifts on his feet, as if trying to prepare himself for the question I could ask next. Will they be honest? Are they ready to be open with me? Am *I* ready to learn the truth behind the Grimm Brothers?

Chapter Twenty

Rhys

"Could we start at the beginning? I know when you met, but I don't know anything about any of your pasts. I've been assuming, or guessing, at bits and pieces but I want to know how you three ended up like...this." She hesitates on the word, but despite the care with which she's asking, her prying questions rip through the room like stray bullets searching for their targets.

My brothers are stiff and vulnerable to the demons beginning to tear through their minds. Xander's eyes are dark. Empty. He's lost, drowning in one of the many horror stories that plagued his childhood, and Everett's posture is rigid despite obvious efforts to seem unaffected.

I pull Brielle tighter into my side, stroking a thumb over her hip as worry creases her forehead. She's worried she's overstepped. She's worried that her prying is causing more damage than the good understanding us would bring. While I want to ease her concerns, I'm stranded myself, anxious that what she'll learn will be more than she can bear. We are monsters, after all.

"None of our childhoods were pretty, Flower," I finally murmur, breaking the uncomfortable silence that has begun to suffocate the room. Everett's lips thin, and I know without him having to argue that he doesn't agree with what I said. He's heard Xander's and my screams in the night. He doesn't believe that his childhood, despite the hell he survived, was bad enough to cause any damage. He doesn't realize that, no matter how tame his past may be compared to mine or Xander's, he still had to survive a hell no child should have to endure. "Are you sure?"

"Yes." She nods, the hesitation that had weighed her down earlier, gone. It's in that simple answer that I realize how selfish we've all been with her these past few weeks. We've wanted every piece of her, but we'd not been willing to give her every piece of ourselves. That ends tonight.

"The beginning, huh?" I nuzzle her hair, inhaling the intoxicating scent of her as I allow myself to drift slowly back in time. It's not something I allow myself to do often, but dammit, if she wants me, *all* of me, I'm going to give it to her. "I started along the outskirts of the city, in a trailer park, with my mother."

She's turned slightly so that she can see me better, her large eyes locked on me as she listens, her chest barely moving as if she's too afraid of what's to come to breathe. *I know I am.* What if this changes us? Sure, it could be for the better, but what if it's for the *worse*? What if she never looks at us the same way again?

I force a breath past the tightness in my chest and grit my teeth before continuing. "She was a crack whore. She'd sell herself for whatever drugs she could get her hands on and when her body wasn't enough to pay the price of her addiction, she'd sell mine, too."

Brielle jolts as if she's been struck, her face paling as my words settle onto her shoulders, weighing them down. I'm almost unsure if I should continue, unwilling to drag her into the depths of my world, but she nods, silently urging me to continue.

"Her dealers used and abused me for a long time. Eventually, the state got involved but, by then, a lot of the damage was already done." I look down at my hands, still singed and pink from the fire I'd set to that bar, and shake my head. "I was eight when they placed me in my first foster home. Too young to hunger for the kind of revenge I'd been craving, but starving for it nonetheless."

Everett shifts, already knowing where this story goes and how it ends, his knuckles white from the anger that's clamped them shut. He hates remembering, or being reminded of our pasts. If he could, I know he'd travel back in time, desperate to save two boys from the damning lives lurking in their futures.

"When I was ten, I finally had the opportunity I'd been waiting for. I had all of the names of the johns who'd beat me, all of the addresses of the men who'd sodomized me and dealt out those drugs to my mother. More importantly, I knew how I was going to kill them."

Again, I pause, searching Brielle's face for a sign that she's not ready for me to continue. When I find nothing, I keep going. "I'd wait until they were just starting to enjoy their addiction of choice—whether that be alcohol, meth, or cocaine—to sneak into their houses. I'd douse the ground level with gasoline and, when they were too far gone to fight back, I'd tie them up and soak them with whatever I had left." The ghost of a smile flickers across my lips as I reach into my pocket and pull out my lighter, a gift I'd received on my last birthday with my mother. I flick it open, tilt it, and allow a small lick of flame to drop into my palm, searing the skin with a delicious burn that causes my breath to catch in my throat. "I watched them burn until their homes, their lives, and their legacies were *nothing.*"

I flick the lighter closed with a slow breath and lift my eyes to meet Brielle's. I expect them to change. To fill with disgust, anger or fear. Instead, they're brimmed with tears, understanding, and...*love.* She reaches toward me and takes my seared hand in hers, a single tear working free as she lifts my hand to her lips and presses a gentle kiss to my burn. I choke out a loud breath, unsure if I want to laugh or cry. Other than the two men standing above us, I've never met anyone so accepting of *me.*

"By the time I'd made it through my list, I'd landed myself in a group home for troubled boys in the city with a nickname that branded me like I'd branded each one of those men," I finish.

"Blaze." Brielle's soft voice startles me out of the memory, and I nod, shrugging my shoulders.

While I'd prefer to forget the reason I earned my nickname, I know that my past is the reason I ended up where I am today. With my brothers and Brielle.

"What happened to your mother?" she asks, her fingers tracing along the back of my hand.

I wince, unable to control the automatic response that comes with the reminder of her death.

"She overdosed the night the state removed me from my home. I'll never know if it was accidental, or…" I trail off, allowing my silence to fill in the blanks.

Or if she killed herself.

"I'm sorry." It's the first time anyone has ever offered me any condolences for her death, and I'm uncertain how to react as I nod mechanically in thanks.

I'd been so preoccupied with revenge in my youth that I hadn't allowed myself the time to ponder what her death meant for me, or how it made me feel. What was I truly losing with her passing? The woman had never acted as a mother should, and she'd certainly never provided me with the safety a growing child needs, but she'd still been my *mom*.

"You're allowed to be sad that she's gone, Rhys. You're allowed to be *happy* that she's gone, too," Brielle murmurs, the gentle words making my heart ache painfully in my chest.

How does this woman know me so well?

I kiss her forehead and allow her presence to pull me out of my thoughts. Away from my mother, the johns, and the storm… I close my eyes, take a deep breath, and force myself to remain in the present. To remain here, in this room, with my family. The family we made for ourselves.

And fuck, there isn't anywhere else I'd rather be.

Chapter Twenty-One

Brielle

I blink at Rhys and force back the tears that threaten to spill as I shift closer to him, wrapping my arms around his neck so I can pull him in for a small hug. He's stiff, but the second I drop my head into the crook of his neck he melts, tugging me into his lap and turning me to face his brothers.

"Well, boys, my turn's over." Rhys forces out a stiff laugh as he leans around me, his hands stroking over my thighs as he looks between me and the two remaining Grimm Brothers. "You're up."

Xander and Everett share a look, a silent conversation passing between their unreadable faces. While it's isolating not being able to understand what they're telling one another, it's also astonishing to see the connection that these men share. *Maybe we'll get there one day, too.*

"I want you to know that my childhood was docile, compared to my brothers." Everett steps forward, and gestures around the room. "I grew up homeless, but I had my parents. I never knew when I'd get my next meal, but I was enrolled in school."

Like it was with Rhys' story, my mind is filled to the brim with questions I know I can't ask. *Where are his parents now? Where did he live, if not in a home? How long did he have to go hungry?* I want to know it all, but I have to be patient. I need to listen and see what pieces of himself he's willing to share with me before I go prying any further. This is already pushing them way past the fading line that had been drawn between us when I first arrived in their home.

"My parents *tried*. Which is more than any kid can really ask for." He stops, his Adam's apple bobbing up and down as he swallows, and I wonder for a moment if that's all he's willing to delve into his background. He looks at Rhys, and it's in that small glance that I spot the guilt darkening his brown gaze as he shifts on his feet. "I lost them both to pneumonia when I was twelve, after a really rough fucking winter..."

My heart thumps unsteadily as he grits his teeth, biting back the pain this memory causes.

"For some reason, I survived. The hospital that couldn't save them saved me, cleaned me up, and turned me over to social services once I was strong enough to be released." He smirks then, a subtle hint of joy crossing his features as he readies the next part of his story. "My first day at the new school, I ran into this scrawny, blond-haired kid who looked about as dead on the inside as I felt."

Rhys laughs, the light sound almost unfitting amongst the stories that have filtered through this room tonight. "Who're you calling scrawny? We were the same fucking size."

A harsh chuckle escapes Xander before he has the chance to stop it, the light smile tugging up the corners of his lips disappearing as quickly as it had appeared.

"He got us both into a lot of trouble, but I was glad to have him around. He was a positive *light* that kept me from looking back." The gratitude on Everett's expression is heartwarming, but I can't shake the feeling of trepidation brewing in the air. "I joined the army after I aged out of the system at eighteen. In my first year, I managed to rank above my class, and by the time we were deployed, I was a corporal."

His discipline, respect for the rules, and loyalty are beginning to make more sense now. The complicated puzzle that is the Grimm Brothers is slowly beginning to come together.

"I lost myself, overseas." His confession is a shocking twist that I wasn't expecting. I tense in Rhys' arms, ready for the boot to drop. "It wasn't the war, the gunfire, or the bombings that got to me, though. It was these two kids…" He reaches into his pocket and pulls out his pair of brass knuckles, a weapon I've witnessed him use to crush another man's jaw. "Their dad was beating them, raping them, and forcing them into prostitution, and we were just supposed to *ignore* it."

I shiver, an unexpected sweep of fear and disgust chilling me to the core.

"I tried. I had orders to follow and, unfortunately, those orders didn't include looking out for those kids." He slides the brass knuckles over his hand and lifts the deadly metal to inspect it before continuing. "We were only a few days from pulling out of that town. I was so close to putting that family behind me, when the father approached me, and offered me his daughter for the night. She was only ten, Brielle. Ten."

I can see the distress beginning to contort his features, hear it in the way he emphasizes her age and again, I wonder if I'm pushing them too far. Asking for too much.

"I told him I wanted to discuss—" He pauses, and swallows. "*Pricing*...somewhere more private."

I wince at the imagery, hating the hurt and anger that must have plagued him from carrying the burden of pretending to comply with that girl's torture.

"So, I invited him back to our encampment. When he got there, I knocked him out, and chained him up in one of our cellars. I hung him there until he'd pissed and shit on himself, and when I was satisfied that he felt as defenseless as his daughters, I beat him." He scratches at a noticeable scuff in the metal on his brass knuckles. "By the time they pulled me off him, his skull was caved in and there was nothing left of him to save."

"Shame," Xander mutters, and it's the first time that he's spoken since his brothers started sharing.

If it weren't for his overwhelming size and presence taking up most of the opposite wall, I'd almost have believed he'd disappeared into the floorboards.

"His children were orphans because of me, but at least they were free. That man, he was the first I'd ever killed in cold blood, and in his death, Brass was born. They dishonorably discharged me because of my actions, and losing control over my life like that, like I had when I was younger, threw me into a spiral. I was so *angry*." Everett turns and nods to Xander, who pushes himself away from the wall to hover close beside his brother. "Xander and Rhys saved me from myself."

I glance between the three of them, the Grimm Brothers, whose mysteries are slowly beginning to unravel. I'm starting to understand, but I still have so many questions. My eyes meet Xander's, their blue color still as breathtaking as they'd been the first time I'd seen them, and I can only hope that they hold the answers I'm still searching for.

Chapter Twenty-Two

Xander

What am I doing? Not for the first time since Brielle's arrival into our lives, I find myself questioning the man I am, the man that I'm becoming, and the man that I want to be. My father made it his personal mission to ensure that every possible emotion and weakness was beat out of me while he was alive, and yet, standing in this house, I realize that Brielle is changing me, again. I *want* to share my past with her. I want to unload some of the horrors that've weighed me down for years, but, every fiber of my being is screaming at me to shut down. To throw up my walls, get angry, and do my best to forget. How can one person change years of lessons, discipline, and hell?

I straighten my shoulders, feeling stiff and rigid, and slowly meet the hazel eyes that've been waiting patiently to greet mine. I can see the confusion in her gaze, the worry and fear that I'll shut her out again buried underneath the surface. What if this is too much for her to handle?

"I don't want you to carry my demons, Amour." My words make her frown, and she shifts in Rhys' lap, preparing for a dismissal. "But I gave you my word that I'd try. If this is really what you want…"

"It is," she confirms before I have the chance to question her further. She leans forward, providing me with her undivided attention as my brothers lift their eyes to me, needing to see if I'm ready to let her in. *What choice do I have?* I promised I wouldn't shut her out anymore.

"My father was a cruel man." It's the biggest understatement of the century. *Cruel* doesn't even begin to cover the horrors that fucker put me through. Monstrous. Savage. Brutal. Inhumane. All of the words that come to mind, all of the words in the fucking dictionary, will never be enough. "I do not have a single happy memory from my childhood."

I don't want her sympathy, I just…want her to understand what created the man — the monster — standing before her today.

"My mother died when I was young. I'm not sure what happened to her — whether she got sick, or if he killed her, but I always knew better than to ask… She was gone by the time I turned three, and what little memories I did have of her, my father twisted." Thinking back on it now, I realize that somewhere along the beatings and the torture, my father erased her image from my mind. I can't remember what she looked like, or how she sounded. She must have had an accent — the woman migrated from France when she was a teenager — but was it thick, or had it lessened during her time in the States? "The punishments he would come up with were designed to kill any emotion or attachment I could ever fathom forming. He tried to keep things original, but the fucker favored a belt."

A slice of pain cuts through my back, a phantom belt delivering a painful blow that makes me shudder where I stand.

"He raised me to be a killer, Amour. A Beast he could control and use to rule his empire." Something tugs deep inside me with my admittance, and I can't bring myself to meet Brielle's gaze. "He would've gotten his way if I hadn't met my brothers."

I look between the two men, and while our differences are notable, it's our similarities that draw my attention. We've overcome. We've grown. We're changing. *For her.*

"He was trying to teach me when he sent me to tour the school that day. He wanted me to see how weak my generation was. How pliable, and expendable." I roll my shoulders. "That lesson would turn out to be my father's undoing and…eventually, it would be what led to his death."

That day is a vivid memory that stirs pain, anger, fear and, strangely, above all else, happiness. My father never anticipated his puppet would grow tired of having a hand shoved up their ass, but he'd finally pushed me too far. Demanded too much. How could I kill them? The two boys who'd found me in the deepest pits of hell and were fighting to pull me out? I'd spent years hiding their existence from him, but he noticed — of course he noticed — the strings of control he'd had over me snapping. Being cut. That's what my brothers were doing. *Cutting me free of him.*

The order came through after a thorough lesson about respect. I'd gone against him, harboring friendships with Rhys and Everett. I'd grown too attached, and that attachment would be to the detriment of his empire. He wouldn't allow me the weakness that came with caring relationships.

Kill them.

His voice echoes through my head, and I shudder, my eyes locking onto the hazel orbs in front of me, grounding me as I continue.

"I remember the shock that crossed his face when I drove my knife into his stomach. I remember his tears, and his pleas for mercy when I slit his fucking throat." I look down at my hands, and can almost imagine his blood on them again. "Killing him didn't free me like I'd dreamt it would. That freedom I'd been longing for came to me in pieces." I pause, and gesture to Rhys, Everett, and finally, down at her. "I understand how we found each other, Amour. Darkness attracts darkness. But you…? You confuse me. I can't fathom how a ray of fucking sunshine like you ended up with the three of us."

She blinks up at me for a moment, silently contemplating her answer before she stands. She crosses the room and wraps her arms around me before I have the chance to anticipate her actions.

"Light and darkness can't exist without each other." She pulls away as she speaks, glancing over her shoulder to smile back at Rhys and Everett. I'm ready for her to pull away when she stands up on her toes, and whispers so only I can hear, "I'm going to chase away your darkness, Xander. I promise."

Chapter Twenty-Three

Brielle

Xander's arm remains around me as I turn to face the room again. Rhys and Everett are watching our interaction with a mixture of what looks to be curiosity and hope. I try to tamp down the heat that creeps up my neck as I glance between them.

"Is...there anything you guys want to know?" I ask.

It only seems fitting that it be my turn to open up after all the stories they've shared with me tonight, but will they want me to? What if they have no interest in getting to know me as deeply as I now know them?

"I want one happy memory from your childhood," Xander replies.

He releases my hip and I sink back to the floor beside Rhys, my mind conjuring thousands of moments from the time I'd spent in this house, but none of them good. Will Samuel struggle like this? Will he be able to think of a happy memory on demand, or will he remember a childhood filled with poverty, danger, and me struggling to keep us afloat?

"My mother was a librarian." The words tumble out of my mouth, and as I speak, I imagine her in the space with us. She's wearing her favorite sweater, and her hair hangs loosely around her shoulders with a singular gray streak framing her face. "We used to spend a lot of time together at the library, even when she wasn't working. We'd read, do homework..."

I trail off as the picture I'd conjured of her begins to fade, disappearing like the sun during a storm. It's been so hard, trying to remember how she'd been before her illness ravaged her body. It's easy to forget that before she'd become sick and frail, we'd looked nearly identical.

"She used to let me stamp some of the books at checkout, and once, I met an author who wrote and illustrated his own children's books. I begged him for a signed copy and never touched it again. I didn't want to ruin its value." I giggle now, remembering how I'd stretched from her lap to reach the book she'd laid on the counter for him to sign.

I used to fit so perfectly there, in her arms. In the end, though, it was her that fit in mine.

"Is she why you wanted to become a librarian?" Everett asks.

My eyes drag to where he stands and I nod, my face flushing with warmth. He remembered?

"Yes. A librarian, or the owner of some quirky bookstore in the city," I confirm.

"But you're an RN?" The confusion in Xander's voice is mirrored on Rhys' face.

I shift a little, knowing that previously when we'd touched on this topic, I'd tip-toed around providing an answer. Now? I guess it's finally time.

"I got my nursing degree because I needed to be sure—" I pause and swallow around the lump that's formed in my throat. "I needed to be sure that I'd know what to do if someone I loved was dying in front of me. I couldn't... I can't sit by and watch it happen, not again."

I shake my head and shrug, my eyes jumping between the brothers as I attempt to read them. Rhys reaches out to stroke my knee, and I sniff, forcing back the sadness creeping over me.

"I'm glad. If you hadn't, I'd probably be fucking dead."

Xander's response earns a sharp look from Everett, and Rhys stiffens, his mouth parting to reply when I laugh. A real, body-quaking laugh.

It tips me over, and I lie on my back, looking up at Xander with a giggle. "Lucky you."

"Lucky me." He nods.

"Lucky us," Rhys corrects, lying down beside me. "We're all lucky to have you, Flower."

I smile. Yes, I may not be where I imagined myself but this? This is so much better. I'll trade anything, do anything if it means I get to have them.

All of them.

* * * *

I'm not sure when it happened, when the house that had once been my prison became my home but, I realize on the slow trek up the winding drive, that I'm glad to be back. The dread, fear, and regret that had once filled my bones at the mere thought of entering this house again is gone. I *want* to be here, in this house, with these men. *My* men. Knowing their stories, their backgrounds, and the truth behind each one of them, has only solidified the connection I feel to them. *How can I go back to my family, now?*

"I've still got to make my rounds. You guys head on in. I'll be back around midnight." Xander has pulled up to the front of the house, his grip on the steering wheel tight as his blue eyes find mine in the rearview mirror. "You should try and get some sleep, Amour."

I nod and offer him a small smile as I lean forward between the seats.

"Stay safe. For me...okay?" I press a gentle kiss to his bearded cheek, surprising him, and myself, as Rhys opens up the back door beside me. I slip out of the car, taking Rhys' hand so he can help me down, and giggle as his green eyes jump from me to the man sitting frozen behind the steering wheel.

"I think this is the first time I've ever seen him speechless," Rhys murmurs into my ear, a loud chuckle slipping through his parted lips as we turn toward the front door.

"It's a good look on him." I muse, glancing back at the car, where Everett is still sitting in the passenger seat. His eyes are downcast, and his lips move as he and Xander share a conversation we aren't meant to be privy to. *What are they talking about...?*

"Nosy little thing, aren't you?" Rhys is at my ear again, his dark chuckle the only warning I have before he moves, spinning me and pinning me up against the front door. I flush, embarrassed to have been caught, and look up at him through my lashes.

"Are they okay?" I whisper, biting into my lower lip as he cages me in with his long arms, his blond waves cascading around his cheeks.

"They're all right, Flower. There's a lot we didn't unpack tonight, about Xander's hand in Everett's life. I think he's just expressing his thanks. We'll explain it to you one day, Brielle, just not tonight. We've uncanned enough worms for now." He reaches down and strokes a thumb along my bottom lip, freeing it from between my teeth with a distractingly tantalizing touch that *melts* me.

"You're doing that on purpose." My voice is breathier than I intend, and he laughs lightly at my reaction, leaning away from me with that devilish grin so he can open the door.

"It's working, isn't it?" His lips find mine as he pulls me into the house, a low growl of pleasure leaving the back of his throat as our mouths begin to explore one another. "Fuck, you're so goddamn addictive, Flower."

I tug at his shirt, powerless against the spark of pleasure beginning to take root in my stomach, and pull him closer, groaning as his tongue traces my lower lip. My head swims, and I moan, pressing into his chest as his steady hands snake around my body, the heat from his skin enough to twist a wave of need deep within my core. *Fuck, I want him.*

A small warning chirp sounds from the alarm behind us as it's deactivated, distracting us long enough to see that Everett has returned from the car, his brown eyes burning with heat. "Please, don't let me interrupt." His lips curl up into a delicious smile that makes my stomach curl with anticipation. "I just hope you know you aren't keeping her to yourself."

Fuck, I want them both.

Rhys chuckles, his grip on me loosening just enough that he's able to turn me in his arms, facing me outward so that my eyes are now locked with Everett's. "Was that a request, or an order, *sir*?"

Sir...? I almost shake at the sound of that honorific coming from Rhys' tongue, my entire body tensing as I wait, anxiously, to see how Everett will respond. He's grinning, his dark eyes unmoving from mine as he crosses the room toward us, his fingers reaching out to skate across my jaw once he's reached us.

"Would you like to play, pet?" His voice is a low growl that would drop me to my knees if not for Rhy's arms, still secured around my body. *How do these men always know what I need?*

"Yes, sir." My voice is so small it's almost eaten by the surrounding room, my need evident as I press back into Rhys' budding erection.

"What do you think, Blaze? Your room, or mine?" Everett's fingers slip down my throat, his brown orbs tracing over my body as if his gaze alone can devour me. *Maybe it can.*

"Mine." Rhys releases me with a slow stroke of his hands down my body, his large grin matched only by the excitement lighting up Everett's eyes. Fuck. *What do these men have in store for me?*

Chapter Twenty-Four

Rhys

Nothing will ever be a better distraction than Brielle, naked and bare in front of us. *This woman is going to be our undoing.*

I'm straddling her, admiring her body, and waiting patiently while Everett fishes a pair of restraints from the chest of toys by my closet. It's not much of a collection, just enough to keep things entertaining, but for Brielle, it's going to be the beginning of an entirely new world of pleasure.

She's watching me, her skin covered in goosebumps as she shivers beneath my steady gaze, her chest rising and falling in quick, uneven movements. She's nervous, but excited, too. *It's just the way we like her.*

"Close your eyes, Flower," I instruct, smirking with delight as her eyelids flutter shut. Everett has appeared beside the bed, a pair of fuzz-covered handcuffs pinched in his grasp, and I chuckle as I begin to slide off her body. The cuffs, although made of metal, are flimsy enough that if she tried hard enough, she could break out of them. They're definitely a better starting place than the rope or police-grade cuffs that I have on standby in case anyone is feeling…adventurous.

"Arms above your head, pet." His rumbled command has barely left his lips before she's moving, her slender arms quick to rise above her head.

"What a good girl," I purr, unable to contain the excitement her submission stirs within me. Sure, Everett may be the dominant of our group, but all of us can, and do, enjoy a woman that's submissive in the bedroom.

Everett is slow as he moves to lean over her, drawing out her anticipation as he drags a finger up her arm, caressing her, and soaking her in before he clasps a delicate wrist between the cuff. She gasps.

"The safe words are yours to use at your discretion," he reminds her, grinning as she begins to chew on her lower lip. He loops the cuffs through the rails of my bed, and binds her other wrist, linking her to the headboard, and trapping her in the center of the bed. "Do you understand, pet?"

"Yes, sir." She nods and tugs at the restraints keeping her laid out for us to use at our disposal, testing their strength. When they don't budge, a small moan brushes past her parted lips, and I chuckle as her little mewl of pleasure jolts my cock to life in my pants.

"Are you up for putting on a show, Blaze?" Everett's low question slips to me from where he stands beside the bed, his attention divided between me and the woman lying in front of him. I can see the excitement burning through his eyes, the hunger that's growing in their brown depths. *Am I up for putting on a show?*

"Your wish is my command, sir." The answer is simple enough to find.

Bowing slightly, I smile as he lowers himself into the wingback chair diagonal to the bed and waits. His dominant side is ready to take control, and I am ready to let him have it.

"Fuck her with your mouth, Blaze. Make her come. I want to hear her scream." His demands make Brielle shiver, a low whimper clawing from her chest as I nod and climb onto the bed.

Brielle is watching me through hooded eyes, her thighs parted just enough to grant me a glimpse of her gloriously wet pussy. The sight is enough to harden my cock even further, and I groan as she spreads her legs wider, willingly and unashamedly opening herself up to me. *Fuck, she's gorgeous.*

"Taste her." Everett's voice is a rough drawl that makes Brielle squirm below me, her short, controlled, breaths only growing more vigorous as I begin positioning her to my liking below me.

With one leg over my shoulder, and one pinned beneath my arm, not only is she at a better angle for Everett, but she's also in a position that will ensure that *I* can keep her spread open for me. Once I'm satisfied, I don't waste another fucking minute.

I swear, I will never get tired of the taste of this woman. As soon as I dip my tongue into her center, the sweet taste of her arousal explodes across my tastebuds, and I groan, desperate for more. I drag my tongue through her folds, soaking up the desire that has already begun to seep from her and circle her clit, humming in pleasure as she quivers beneath me.

"Fuck, Rhys." She groans as I swirl my tongue around the sensitive bundle of nerves again, dipping my hand between her legs so I can slip an index finger inside her. "Oh, *god.*"

I wrap my lips around her clit, trapping it between my teeth as I swirl my finger inside of her, stroking her G-spot and pulling her closer to the edge of climax. She can barely contain her moans. *She's so fucking breathtaking.*

"Two fingers, Blaze. I want her ready to take your cock." Everett's grunted command falls into the space between us, and when I glance toward him, I can see that he's fisted his dick, his large hand moving in slow languid movements that match my own. *Fuck.*

"Yes, sir." I ease another digit into her cunt, a groan lashing from my chest as she rolls against my hand, desperate for more friction. I push into her, matching the pace of her hips as they move, but I ease up on her clit, enjoying the mewl of frustration that ebbs from her throat.

"Rhys, please." I can feel her walls beginning to squeeze around me, a telltale sign that she's close to bridging the short climb between pleasure and ecstasy, but I don't relent, my tongue drawing small circles around her.

"You're asking the wrong brother, Flower," I murmur, meeting her hooded gaze with a devilish grin that has her head dropping back against the mattress.

"Can I come? Please, sir?" Her legs are beginning to quake around me, despite having let up on the swollen clit in front of me. "What was that, pet?" Everett is enjoying the sight of her squirming, almost as much as I'm enjoying being the cause of her squirming.

"Please, sir, may I come? Please?" She's borderline begging now, her face contorted with the concentration it's taking not to come apart around me. Fuck, her begging is enough to make *me* want to explode.

"Yes, pet. You may come." The second that he relents, I pull her clit back into my mouth again and suck, hard. It's only a beat later that she screams out her pleasure, her walls clamping around my finger as I continue to suck her clit, dragging out her orgasm until her body is tense and wound tight again with desire. Only then, do I pull my mouth away from her pussy.

"Fuck, Flower," I breathe, dragging my tongue around my lips as I rise to kneel above her, ensuring not a drop of her release is left behind. "You're so fucking beautiful when you come apart like that."

"I think she's nice and warmed up now, Blaze. Fuck her. Fuck her and get her ready for me." Everett's husky growl makes Brielle flush, and she bites into her lower lip as I raise my brow at her, watching her reaction.

"Well, Flower? Would you like that?" I whisper, leaning down to press my lips to hers. She's so soft, I can't help but melt into her, my erect cock pressing against her thigh as she wraps her legs around me.

"Yes. Fuck me, Blaze, please. I want your cock inside me."

Chapter Twenty-Five

Brielle

"Yes. Fuck me, Blaze, please. I want your cock inside me."

A normal woman, with pride and dignity, wouldn't beg or fall apart like this in front of two men. I know that I'd craved it, that sense of normalcy in my life, but I'm slowly beginning to realize that I'm no longer *normal* myself. These men have changed me. My experiences have changed me. Despite whatever yearning I'd felt earlier, I don't think I can imagine a piece of normal that's better than this, ever again.

I pull at my restraints again, testing their durability. I'm sure if I struggled hard enough, the flimsy, fabric-covered metal would break, but something is intriguing — albeit mildly frustrating — about being bound. While my hands itch to race through Rhys' hair and help him out of his clothes, my core is throbbing with the excitement and danger my vulnerability has created. *What is wrong with me?*

"Please fuck me," I whisper, my face heating from the embarrassment. I know this is all still new, but I'm sure other women don't plead like this. *Right?*

"What a naughty little thing." Rhys' voice is a low growl in my ear as he pulls away from me, straightening enough that he's able to begin shedding his clothes. He's beautiful. Hell, these men are *all* breathtaking. The moment his shorts come off, his cock springs toward me, and I find myself whimpering with the need to have him inside me. I squeeze my thighs together, attempting to relieve some of the pressure.

"It looks like our pet is getting impatient, Blaze." Everett's gravelly voice draws my attention to where he sits across the room, and I groan in frustration when I see him. His brown eyes are hooded with lust, and his hand is working in slow, rhythmic movements over his cock, pumping it and drawing forth a delicious-looking bead of pre-cum. Why isn't that *my* hand?

I open my mouth, ready to complain, when Rhys begins to settle over me, his muscular chest flattening against my breasts. His skin is a warm distraction, and I almost forget to breathe as the head of his rock-hard cock presses against my center. One small thrust, and he'll be inside of me.

"Are you ready, Flower?" His lips find mine again, and I nod without breaking our contact, my hips lifting on their own in an attempt to guide him inside me. He chuckles, our mouths a combative mess of desperation and desire as he reaches between us to finally guide himself in. I nearly come from the mere feeling of him spreading me, his rock-hard length penetrating and filling me up almost too much to bear in my frenzied state. I want *more.*

He slides out of me, the movement slow and torturous, before thrusting back in, the sporadic jolt driving the air from my lungs in a long and boisterous moan. "Fuck, Blaze."

He chuckles, his trimmed beard scratching delicately against my skin as he begins to kiss along my jawline, his hips moving at a new, and even pace. It's exhilarating, and so filling, that I can hardly contain the excited mewls that spill from me.

"I know she can take more than that, Blaze. Fuck her harder!" Everett barks, his husky demands causing Rhys to drive into me harder, and faster. I pant out rushed breaths, my heart slamming as my pleasure begins to build again, another wave of climax cresting just beyond the horizon.

"Oh, god." I clutch at the rails of the bed as he shifts his hips, allowing his pelvis to strike my clit with each thrust.

"It's not God making you feel this good, Flower. Say my name." Rhys growls through clenched teeth as he continues his unrelenting rhythm, one hand dropping between us to pinch my clit between his fingers.

"Rhys!" I cry out as I come, this climax somehow more intense than the last. I convulse around him, my body twitching with my release as he pushes harder, chasing his orgasm.

"Fuck, Brielle," he curses as he pulls out of me, his hand quick to replace my pussy as he comes, his warm, sticky ejaculate spreading across my lower stomach. I moan at the sensation, my body a tight knot of sated pleasure as he sinks back against his heels with a lopsided grin. "So fucking perfect."

I blush, my body warm and weak. I could sleep, but as I blink my heavy eyes, Everett appears beside the bed, his own cock stretched out and hard for me. *Can I really come again?*

"Ready for me, pet?" he asks, grinning as Rhys shifts out of the way. I'm breathless, sweaty, and tired, but fuck if seeing his cock hard for me isn't enough to stir another round of desire through me.

"Yes, sir." I lick my lips, moistening them as he climbs onto the bed, his cock so hard it almost looks painful. I still can't believe something that size can fit into me.

"I'd like to try something new. If you really are willing to take on all three of us, your body is going to need some training before it's ready to accommodate us at one time." He holds up a small black toy, the circular end pinched between his fingers. "Do you know what this is?"

I may be new to sex, but I've heard and seen more than enough in my classes to make an educated guess. "A butt plug?"

"Yes." He nods, and squishes the tip between his index finger and thumb, showing me how pliable it is. "I'd like to use this to see if anal play is something you're even vaguely interested in. If it's not, I'll remove it, and the subject will be off the table unless you change your mind. Is that okay?"

I'm nodding before he's even finished speaking. I've always been willing to try something once, and if this little piece of silicone is something that can get me closer to pleasing them all on my own, I'm more than ready to make that leap. I want their pleasure all to myself. "Yes, sir."

"Remember your safe words." The reminder slips from him as Rhys reappears beside the bed, offering up a bottle of lubricant. Everett takes it his eyes on me and applies it to the small silicone bulb. "Bend your knees, pet, and get ready for me."

I do as he instructs, bending my knees as he presses his free hand against my pussy. His fingers delicately trace my oversensitive bundle of nerves, and I jump as pleasure sears through my body again, a hot lance that I hope never diminishes. As he plays with my clit, he presses the bulb against my ass, gently applying pressure until the bulb slips inside. It's uncomfortable for a second, but as soon as he pushes a finger inside me, the embarrassing pressure blooms into... something more. Something pleasurable. *Fuck, I like this.*

"*Oh,*" I moan, a rush of air leaving my lips as he shifts, one hand remaining on and working my clit while the other pumps his shaft.

"Remember to breathe, pet." His warning barely registers before he's slipping inside me, the feeling of him and the plug at once, almost too much to bear. "Breathe, Brielle."

I do as he says, pulling in a large breath as he begins to move, drawing his hips back slowly before pressing himself into me again.

"Brass!" I moan, my hips bucking. *Is this too much? Should I safeword?*

It's as I'm nearly ready to cave that my body relaxes, accepting the intrusion of them both, and sending a fresh tidal wave of pleasure through my body. It's a more intense, fuller, pleasure than I've ever experienced, and I find myself dancing along the lines of oblivion again.

"Brass, oh fuck," I cry out, my moans so loud my throat is beginning to feel raw.

"You like this, pet?" Everett has picked up his pace, his jaw tight as he rocks into me, his own pleasurable grunts filling the bedroom.

"Yes! Yes, sir." I nod, gripping the rails of the bed again as the pressure and pleasure build, making me scream. "Everett!"

"Hold on, pet," he grits, gripping my waist. Before I realize what's happening, he's turning me, flipping me onto my stomach and pulling me up by my hips so I'm on my knees.

My hands are tangled in the cuffs, and the metal bites into my skin, but that only increases my pleasure, my body rocking back against him as he begins thrusting into me again. *Oh, fuck.* I'm already so close. *How is that possible?* I can't come again. It's impossible...isn't it?

"You're getting so tight, pet. Fuck," Everett curses under his breath, his fingers clutching my skin, as his pace increases.

"I'm close." I pant, another moan ripping from me as he sheathes himself to the hilt, his cock stretching and hitting me so deep, I can't help the lewd shouts that escape me.

"Come for me, Brielle." His order comes out in a tight rasp as he reaches around me to find my clit with his fingers. He strokes me, and after a tantalizing beat, I feel the wave beginning to crash around me.

"Oh, Everett!" I cry, beginning to shake as an orgasm rips through me. My walls clamp down around him, and I feel him surge, pressing himself harder, and faster until he's on the brink himself. He pulls out, and in the same motion removes the butt plug from my ass, the feeling of it leaving my body increases the orgasm. He comes, his cum spreading across my ass, and I collapse, spent, exhausted, and *so* fucking happy.

"Beautiful, pet." Everett's hand skims my body, massaging away the sting left behind by his grip on my hips. "You're so fucking gorgeous, Brielle."

I turn onto my side as he reaches across me, freeing me from the restraints as Rhys appears by the bedside, a fresh washcloth in his hands. He cleans me while Everett rubs away the indent left behind by the cuffs, and it's as their hands are delicately caressing me, that I find my eyelids fluttering shut, and sleep pulls me under.

* * * *

Lincoln

This is going to be fucking great.

I chuckle as George stumbles away from me, a dirty mess of piss, shit, vomit and blood. He reeks, and his short-sleeved shirt proudly displays the bruised track marks racing up both of his arms. *Just the way D wanted him.*

"Help! Somebody help me." His voice is a ragged sound that scrapes from his throat, and his feet drag against the crumbling pavement as he makes his way up the street. "Please!"

"No one's going to believe you, George," I taunt, my crude laugh making him wince. He sideswipes a trash can, and it clatters to the ground. "They're going to think you're deranged."

"Shut up," he barks, his hands racing across his head as he desperately scans the roadway, the sidewalks, and the buildings, searching for a glimmer of hope in the midst of one of his darkest nights.

"Who's going to believe a filthy fucking drug addict?" The beratement snags his attention, and he turns, stumbling back toward me.

"*You* did this. You and Draven are after my daughter!" He screams as he lunges toward me, the drugs in his system slowing his swings enough that I'm able to dodge him. "You leave her alone! Do you understand me!?"

"What is going on?" Someone shouts from above us, and when I glance up, I can see a tired old man watching us from his window.

"I need help! This man is attacking me!" I call, feigning innocence and fear as I allow one of George's slow punches to land against my gut. I stumble backward, making the blow seem more forceful than it is, and shout out another plea for help. "Call the cops, please!"

"What are you planning? Why does he want her?" George is too lost in his own mind to hear what's going on around him, his bloodshot eyes wet with unshed tears as he continues to stumble forward. "Why can't you people just leave us alone?"

A small gathering is beginning to form on the streets. Men and women have appeared in their doorways or windows, entranced and curious about the shouting going on in front of their homes.

"You're insane!" I shout, holding up my hands in a feeble act of surrender. It's at the sight of my weakness that a few men begin to emerge from their houses, rushing down the sidewalk in a misguided attempt to help.

"Hey, man, you've gotta relax," one is saying, patting George on the shoulder as another steps in front of me.

"You're not listening to me!" He turns on the man now, grabbing him by the shoulders and shaking him. "He kidnapped me! They're after my daughter!"

"You're high!" The man shoves George back, and the meth in his system keeps him off balance enough that he falls to the ground with a roar.

"Why isn't anyone listening to me?" He pounds the pavement with his fists, throwing a temper tantrum like a toddler while the crowd around us grows, men and women with their phones out recording the altercation.

We all stumble backward as George scrambles to his feet, his hands swinging wildly as a police siren sounds in the distance. He latches onto a woman and pulls her close to his face, his meaty, sweaty hands gripping her arms.

"Please, you've got to help me! My daughter, she's in danger," he pleads.

"Get off of me!" she shrieks, a mixture of fear and appall making her voice pitch above his continued rambling.

She's pulled out of his grasp as a cop car pulls up along the sidewalk, the two officers quick to advance on the scene.

George is raving, the words spilling from his mouth too quick and incoherent to understand as he swings his hands again, his face a desperate tangle of anger and embarrassment.

"Sir, we're going to need you to calm down." The larger of the two cops has stepped forward, his arms outstretched in an obvious attempt to cage George in.

"Calm down? How can I calm down? I was kidnapped! My daughter... Just fucking help me!" George throws his fists out, this time striking the large cop in the jaw. It's a quick blur of limbs as he's tackled to the ground, and cuffs are secured around his wrists.

"All right, we'll take it from here. Everyone, go home." The smaller cop is shooing us away like flies as George screams into the night, his veins bulging from his skin as he wrestles beneath the cop.

I smirk as I slink away, knowing that my job is done. *D will be beyond fucking happy.* Check, please.

Chapter Twenty-Six

Brielle

The sun peering in through the slits of the closed curtains is high in the sky when I wake, warm and snuggled in the center of the bed. It's been far too long since I've managed to sleep so peacefully without the help of medication, and waking without that groggy feeling left behind is refreshing. I guess I have my men to thank for that. Well, them and all the orgasms.

I smile to myself and sit up, the happiness that had just begun to peek inside my chest evaporating as my eyes catch on the sheets beneath me. This isn't Rhys' bed. The color and the texture of the duvet are off, and while it's similar to the one I fell asleep on, the difference is striking enough to leave me feeling uneasy. *Where am I?*

"Rhys? Everett!" I shout, and push myself from the unfamiliar bed.

My feet hit the ground and a chill skitters up my spine as the floor beneath them begins to change, morphing from carpet to cement. *What is happening?* My breath has stalled in my lungs, and my mind races, cataloging each marginally incorrect detail as the drywall melts, transforming into sheets of gray brick. *The basement? When did I come down here?*

I turn in search of the stairs, my frame trembling with adrenaline, and jump when a loud snap comes from behind me. I twist toward the noise and find, not the steps, but an ajar door I've never noticed before. Is it new? Swallowing, I inch toward it, my stomach curling with fear as another crack bounces off the walls.

"Xander...?"

I can see him standing just beyond the opening, his back to me and his shoulders heaving as if he's overexerted himself. *What is he doing?*

I push the door aside and step into the new area silently. This room appears to be a smaller version of the one behind me, but unlike it, this one is void of any items and empty aside from Xander, who still hasn't turned to face me.

"Beast?" My voice is masked by the snap that echoes around us.

I flinch and automatically reach for Xander, but as my fingers grace his elbow, a sickening realization settles over me.

This isn't Xander.

I don't know who he is.

Although he looks to be the same height as my Beast, with the same head full of black curls, this man's body seems almost misshapen when compared to the one I've grown accustomed to. He's atrophied in a way I can't explain, and his muscles are ill-defined beneath his tight clothes. I round him, scanning his wrinkled, angry face.

"Who—" Horror steals my words.

We aren't alone.

A young boy is kneeling in front of the stranger beside me, his exposed back a bloody mess of wounds that crisscross his spine.

"Oh god." I gasp.

Rushing forward, I collapse to my knees in front of the child, my hands searching for additional injuries. I push back his matted hair, cup his cheeks, and lift his chin to scour his face. Ice blue orbs stare back at me.

"Xander?"

Crack.

He winces in my hold and a whimper escapes through his bared teeth. I look behind us, confused, until my eyes lock on the belt in the stranger's hands. *No.*

"Stop." Tears sting my eyes as the man's arm begins to lift, prepared to deliver another blow. "No! Stop!"

Suddenly, I'm standing and shoving the man back. He scrambles away from me with a shout and gags, his hands clawing at his throat. Blood is pouring from a large gash behind them, and he falls to the ground, choking. *How…?* I stare at him, mortified as he struggles to stop the bleeding. I lift my hands, and that's when I see it. The blood. The knife.

No. No, no, no, no, no. No.

I squeeze my eyes shut, stumbling backward as I drop the weapon. I press my hands to my ears, desperate to block out the sounds of the man suffocating on his own blood.

Dreaming.

I have to be dreaming.

I double over, slapping my hands against my cheeks, attempting to tear myself out of the nightmare. *Wake up. I have to wake up!*

Everything grows eerily quiet.

I stay hunched over, nauseated by what I've just witnessed—what I've just done—when a pungent smell begins to assault my senses. My eyes water behind my closed lids from the strength of it surrounding me, and I peel them open to search for the source.

The cement room, the stranger I all but murdered, and Xander are gone. I'm now standing in the middle of a living room while a blond boy circles me, a red fuel can in his hands. He's upturned it and is pouring its contents out on the floor around me, the liquid slicking over the hardwood and soaking it.

Gasoline.

"Rhys...?" I'm confident that's who this is, despite not having a clear view of his face. It's dark, and he doesn't look at me as he continues dousing the surrounding area, ignoring me as if I haven't spoken. "Rhys, what are you doing?"

Music turns on somewhere in the house above us, a pounding bass that makes my body pulse as it vibrates through the walls. It distracts me, and when I turn to look for Rhys again, he's moved to hover outside the front door.

"You won't hurt us again." He holds out his arm, and through the music blasting around me, a distinctive *stsk* echoes in my ears. His lighter. "Burn in hell, fucker."

"Rhys, wait!" I scream, but I'm too late.

An orange flame, the color reflected in his green gaze, falls from his hand to the gasoline spilled at his feet. It catches and ignites, the blast of heat hitting my face as it claws its way into the house.

I shriek, floundering as flames begin to devour the room, licking up the length of the drapes and tearing across the ceiling. It's hot, too hot, and I struggle to breathe as smoke and ashes surround me, filling my lungs.

Screams erupt from above me, and a familiar laugh — Rhys' laugh — comes from the doorway. Flames are spreading toward my feet, and I heave, unable to catch my breath.

This is just a dream.

I have to wake up.

Wake up!

I cough, my lungs screaming, and blink. The heat has evaporated but I'm still choking, my chest heavy with the need for oxygen. White light is blinding me, making my eyes water, and as I shift, I feel something soft below me. *A bed. I'm in a bed?*

My vision is slow to clear, but as it does, I glance around, a nasal cannula tugging at my ears as I twist. Air tickles my nose, but still I can't breathe.

"Everett, can you hear me?" A doctor is beside me, but he isn't addressing me. He's talking to the boy lying in the cot next to mine. "Everett?"

The boy — Everett — moves a hand, but he doesn't utter a response. His brown hair is clumped to his head from sweat, and he coughs, the deep, phlegm-filled hack doing nothing to clear his lungs.

"Your parents… I'm sorry, but they didn't make it." The doctor's voice is gentle as he continues, but it doesn't matter. The blow of his words are devastating despite the kindness he attempts to camouflage them with.

Everett blinks, his skin flushed with fever, and shakes his head. "What?"

"They're gone. I'm so sorry." The doctor repeats the world-shattering news. *No...* "We did everything we could."

He chokes out a sob, and thrashes, ripping at the cords and tubes hooked to him.

Everett...

I reach toward him, wanting to comfort him as nurses swarm the room, but my chest is heavy with the fluid beginning to drown me. I cough, needing to clear my lungs, but it doesn't help. I'm suffocating, asphyxiated by the infection filling my lungs.

This is a nightmare.

I just need to wake up.

Wake up, Brielle.

Now!

I jump, coughing as I come out of the dream, my skin slick with sweat and pebbled from the cold air of Rhys' room. My heat is pounding beneath my ribs, and I'm heaving, attempting to catch my breath as the images slowly recede.

I'm awake. I'm awake.

I fist the sheets and heave in a steadying breath, forcing myself to focus on the physical sensations surrounding me. I need to stay grounded if I'm going to keep myself from having another panic attack.

Inhale, one, two...

I'm cold.

Exhale, three, four...

Air conditioning is blasting from an overhead vent, sending chilled air dancing down along my naked frame.

Inhale, five, six, seven...

I'm sore.

Exhale, eight, nine, ten…

A slight twinge of pain has settled itself between my legs, and my sex is swollen and abused from yesterday's ministrations. It's a good kind of pain, though. One I look forward to welcoming again.

Feeling more at ease, I unwrap my legs from the blankets constricting them and stand, desperate for a shower. Not only am I covered in sweat, my waves clinging to the back of my neck, but my inner thighs still feel sticky with lube despite Rhys' quick wipe down before I'd drifted off. Stretching, I make my way toward the en suite and smile when I find an outfit and fresh towel already laid on the counter for me. How are they always anticipating my needs? It's been so long, and it feels so foreign to have someone care enough about me to predict them. I'm not sure if it's something I'll ever feel used to, but it helps keep my mind occupied as I shower and get dressed.

Once I'm ready, with my wet hair falling freely down my back, I step into the hallway and listen for one of my men. I assume that after pulling a late night, it will be Xander who's home this morning, so I make my way toward his end of the hall.

I'm passing by the office when I hear them, the three hushed voices of the Grimm Brothers, spilling out from behind the cracked door.

I'm about to push into the room, my hand on the door handle, when Xander's roughened whisper breaks across the room, his words stalling me. "When the fuck did this happen? Where is he now?"

His voice is so cold, so deadly, that the hairs on the back of my neck stand as the adrenaline begins to spike through my system, my heartbeat fluttering in my chest.

"Early this morning. He's being held at the local precinct on drug and assault charges. They're shipping him out to the county prison to await sentencing tomorrow." Everett's response is low enough that I can only assume they don't want me overhearing their conversation, my bare feet having been light enough on the carpet to keep my presence unknown. I can't understand why they don't want me to hear. Isn't this *good* news?

My excitement drives me into the room, a hesitant smile pulling up the corners of my lips. "Lincoln's in prison?"

Tears of hope sting my eyes, and my feet feel unsteady beneath me as I cross through the threshold, my heart singing. This is almost over.

I expect to be greeted with their confirming words or nods of affirmation, but as I stand, waiting for a response, I realize I'm only being met with looks of sadness and *pity*. Rhys and Everett are watching me with wide eyes, frozen in place as if they were deer caught in headlights, and it's only then that unease twists through my stomach.

"Come sit down, Amour." Xander's deep, rumbled command snaps my attention to him where he stands by the large window overlooking the front lawn. The leaves are beginning to change on the trees, solidifying the amount of time that's passed since this all began. *Why isn't this over, yet?*

"What's going on?" I'm shaking my head, my inner turmoil making me quake as I realize that the conversation I'd walked in on wasn't about Lincoln.

Certainly, the good news wouldn't be delivered like this.

"It's your father." It doesn't matter how gentle Xander's voice is. It's still enough to send me back a step, my world spinning around me. My father is going to prison? "The police found him this morning after receiving numerous calls about a disturbance. He's being held on multiple accounts of assault and possession with intent to distribute."

It's almost too much for me to comprehend. "My father would never do this…there has to be some mistake."

"This wasn't a mistake, pet." Everett's voice is a tight mixture of anger and sorrow, his dark eyes downcast as realization suddenly strikes me. *This wasn't a mistake.*

"Lincoln did this," I murmur, cringing. Beating him wasn't enough…he had to ruin him, too. Why would he do this? Who would *order* him to do this? *Why are they after my family?*

"Someone recorded the altercation and posted it online. Lincoln was visible in the crowd when the police arrived," Xander confirms, his clenched fist scratching along his jaw. "We'll send men to search the area, but it's likely that the fucker's disappeared again."

"Can I see it?" I whisper, my voice wracked with the tremors tearing through my body. I'm cold. Weak. I want nothing more than to lie in my bed and sleep until all of this is over, but I have to keep pushing. I won't be able to rest until my family is safe again.

Everett is about to unlock the tablet when Rhys shoots a hand forward and snatches it from his brother's grasp, his blond waves twisting wildly as he shakes his head at me. "You don't need to see this, Flower."

"I want to understand—"

"The man in this video isn't your father, Brielle. He may look like him but this isn't George. This man, the man who attacks the people in this video...he's delusional, Flower. He's drugged out of his mind. You don't need that image of him seared into your brain forever." Rhys' words spark a fresh wave of tears to my eyes, and I wither, taking a small step back toward the door.

"We have to do something. He won't last in prison." The tears fall freely down my cheeks now, but I can't back down. We have to come up with a plan to get him out. We have to fix this.

I look to Xander now, anticipating his agreement and willingness to correct the mess my family's in. I'm not prepared for the slow shake of his head that shatters the last shred of hope that had remained for my family's safety.

"I'm sorry, Amour, but we can't—"

"Red." I interrupt him and take another step back, realizing too late that I've surpassed my limit. I need time. More time than my family might have.

"Flower..." Rhys steps forward, arm outstretched, fingers open and reaching for me, but Everett's hand lands on his shoulder, stopping him.

"I-I'm sorry, I just...I can't right now." I feel defeated, my world crashing around me.

"It's okay, pet. Go on." Everett nods toward the door behind me, and I take the opportunity to flee.

My legs give out when I reach my room, and I collapse on the other side of my closed bedroom door, a sob wrenching itself from my throat. First Sammy, and now my father...

Am I going to be the only one left?

Chapter Twenty-Seven

Xander

I grit my teeth as I lower myself into my chair, my hand raking over my face and down the length of my beard. *What the fuck am I going to do?*

"I know she isn't ready to hear this, but prison is probably the safest place for George right now. At least behind bars Lincoln and whatever fuck he's working for can't touch him," I mutter, the beginnings of a headache spreading through my skull. I'm not sure if I'm trying to convince my brothers, of myself, that leaving him behind bars is the best course of action. It wouldn't be hard for Lincoln to find an incarcerated member of his gang to harass George on the inside, but I can't help that feel, instinctually, that his target is shifting. He and his boss, whoever the fucker may be, have never been after George, or Samuel. They're after *her*. "We have to catch these fuckers, and soon."

"We're the only ones standing between her and whoever the fuck is after her." Rhys is boiling, his anger almost palpable. It's rare to see him this worked up, but when it comes to protecting our woman, he's won't stop at anything to ensure that she's safe. *None of us will.*

Everett is pacing, my strategic brother already attempting to formulate a new plan of attack. Before Brielle, I never would have allowed him to interfere or provide any input like this, but now, I can't help but rely on him and his training. She needs us to end this.

When he turns to me, his eyes are dark, and his lips are set in a grim line. He has an idea, but it's not one that he likes.

"Tell me."

* * * *

Draven

A masquerade.

I don't know what kind of idiot The Grimm Brother's think they're dealing with, but they've made this too easy. I smirk as I straighten my mask, my eyes scouring the security guards that patrol the walkway. I'd anticipated this — the additional guns and hired muscle — when I received word of the special theme tonight. It had been far too obvious, that the announcement of their impending attendance — with Rose — was a ploy to lure Lincoln and I out of hiding. They just don't understand who they're underestimating.

"Good evening." A woman greets me from her place behind the counter, her red curls flowing around a fox-shaped mask. "Who do we have here?"

She's scanning me openly, her lips curled into a satisfied grin as I slide my fake ID across the counter toward her. "Gavriel."

She scans the card, and a chirp comes from the computer in front of her as it accesses their system and inputs my information. Information that will be erased as soon as I've finished here.

"Augustin, hmm...? Any relation to that fancy tech billionaire that grew up around here?" She slides the card back to me, hope evident in her features.

"No, I'm afraid not." I laugh.

She frowns, her nails clicking against the keyboard as she types. "That's a shame. Well, it looks like it's your first time with us. What would you like us to call you? Our patrons normally prefer to go by a pseudonym—"

"Gavriel is fine," I interrupt.

I stash the ID back in my pocket and gesture toward the row of elevators in silent question. She smiles and nods.

"Oh, yes, go ahead. If you need anything, just ask one of the staff. Enjoy Once Upon a Time." She plasters that friendly smile back on her face, and moves her attention onto the next person in line.

Pulling out my phone, I input the code that will wipe Gavriel Augustin from their registry and step up to join the crowd waiting to access the levels above us. Hacking into the club's systems is child's play—a simple skill I picked up in elementary school—but deleting their security footage without raising suspicion will be a little more difficult. It's nothing I can't handle, but I'll need to ensure it's done while they're all distracted. I can't risk that someone is watching the feed while it's being wiped. A problem for later.

Blending into the crowd, I step into the elevator once the doors open, and ride up to the third level with the select few that didn't depart for the bar on the second floor. A stage takes up the center of the room, and on it, a woman is being flogged by her partner. The lights are dim, and those that came for the show quickly disperse to find seats. I, however, hang toward the back wall, scanning the room.

Workers are expertly navigating the space, their matching black and white masks helping to distinguish them from other patrons. I wait, doing my best to ignore the sounds coming from the middle of the room, until a male employee heads in my direction.

"Excuse me?" I easily catch his attention.

"Yes, sir?" He's young, and his eyes dart around the room in search of his next task, as if he's desperate to keep busy.

That will work to my advantage.

"Would you be able to procure me a room on the fourth floor?" I keep my voice light, despite knowing the possible argument that's coming.

"Oh, you'll actually need to get a key from the front desk downstairs—"

"It's just that"—I slide forward, and pull my wallet free—"I'd rather not have my show interrupted. I can pay you for the trouble." I flash a stack of hundreds, and the man's jaw goes slack with surprise. He glances around, ensuring that no one is watching, and nods before taking the cash from me.

"What name should I have them put on the reservation?" he asks.

"Timothy Warsaw."

The worker only seems to be half-listening as I provide the name, his eyes too busy scanning the money as he places it into one of his pockets then disappears out a side exit.

Poor kid.

He has no idea what he's just taken part in, but how could he? Timothy isn't a name the workers, or security, here have on their radar tonight. *Idiots.* I sigh, content, as I lean against the wall behind me. Everything is going perfectly, and now? Now, I just need to get things moving. I'm close.

So close, Rose.

* * * *

Xander

I stare at the watch on my wrist, mentally kicking myself as the seconds continue to trickle by. This is a bad idea. I should tell them that the plan is off, that we'll have to find another way to do this, but as I look up the staircase, all of my reasonable thoughts evaporate. Brielle is descending the stairs, and she looks... *Fuck.*

"Will this do?" she asks with a hesitant smile, turning in a small circle once she's reached the bottom step.

I groan as I take her in, all pale skin and curves wrapped in an exposing and sinful black dress. It's a halter neck style, with straps of leather that cut across her chest, drawing my attention to her breasts and the nipples pebbled at their centers. The length drops to the middle of her calves, but just below her ribs, the sides are cut off, leaving only a long strip of fabric to cover her ass and pussy. Leather straps crisscross down her side to the middle of her thighs where they end, allowing the black fabric to float around her body. If the wind catches her just right, she'll be flashing us with that perfect pink cunt. The thought alone is enough to make my cock jerk in my dark-wash jeans.

"*Putain*," I curse, adjusting myself as Everett and Rhys begin to cross through the living room. They're dressed similarly to me, all dark attire, and with Brielle clad in her black dress, we look like we're ready to attend a funeral. *If this works, it's going to end in one.* "Yes, Amour. That'll do."

"Wow, Flower, look at you." Rhys takes her hand once he reaches us and spins her, his green gaze heating with lust as he scans her. It's going to be difficult to keep him on task tonight.

"Are those really necessary?" Brielle questions, her furrowed gaze jumping between us and the guns we're stashing beneath our clothes.

"We're not willing to take the chance that they aren't," Everett replies, stroking a hand down the leather straps at her waist, his wandering touch making her shiver. He's going to be difficult to keep on task, too.

I reach out almost involuntarily and wrap an arm around her, tugging her curvy body back against me as I scan my brothers. Fuck, maybe we're all going to struggle to stay on task tonight. "One of us is to be with her at all times. Understood?"

"Understood," they agree in unison, just as a knock sounds on the front door behind us.

I growl, pulling in a deep breath before I release her, memorizing her scent as I greet Joe, our driver, and head of security for the night. "Is everything in place?"

"Yes. I've got men posted at each entrance, and there's a team canvassing the levels as we speak." He nods, stepping aside so that we can slip into the night.

The air is chilled with the heavy scent of autumn, and I bite back a groan as Brielle brushes past me on Everett's arm, her nipples pebbled from the cold. *Get the job done...then, she's ours.*

The drive to our club is silent. Brielle is sandwiched in the backseat between my brothers, and I'm riding shotgun, my eyes jumping from the world flying by outside our windows, to the tiny woman trapped behind me. Where would she be if we hadn't ever intervened? It's obvious now that George's perceived harm to our business was all an elaborate trap set by Lincoln. They wanted us to kill him. To get him out of the picture. When that didn't happen, they had to come up with another plan. At least for Brielle's sake, this one has kept him alive.

In the week that's passed since George's arrest, we've tried to iron out a plan to weed Lincoln and his boss out of hiding. Everett's idea has been spun and re-thought out a thousand times. We've tried to find a way to keep Brielle out of this, but of course, she always seems to be the missing piece of the puzzle. If she's not there, they won't come for her. And we are overdue for a fucking ending.

"What if he doesn't come?" Brielle's voice breaks into my thoughts, and as her words drag me back, I realize that she's stuck on the same train of thought as me.

"He'll come." I sound more confident than I feel. If Lincoln were smart, he'd steer clear of Once Upon a Time, and us, for the rest of his life. But I'm betting the fucker is starting to get desperate to get Brielle to his boss. "When we announced masquerade night, we made it clear that the Grimm Brothers would be making an appearance. With our Rose."

She's chewing on her lower lip, her eyebrows furrowed over her clouded hazel eyes. I reach back and squeeze her knee, a comforting gesture she's not used to expecting from me. She blinks, and offers me a sideways smile, her fingers running through her curled hair as she tucks it behind her ears.

"They'll stop him before he gets inside?" she asks, eyeing Joe with skepticism.

"He's not going to get near you, pet." Everett's growling promise echoes through the car as we pull into the parking lot of the club, the bright lights outside illuminating the night.

It's crowded. Far more crowded than we anticipated. *This might be more difficult than we anticipated.*

The car stops and Joe slips out first, his eyes scouring the crowd of patrons waiting to get inside. I take the time to turn in my seat, my hand unfurling to reveal a black leather eye mask.

"Put this on, Amour," I tell her, grateful that Mrs. Claebourn had the foresight to match the mask to her dress. She takes it from me and slips it over her head as Joe knocks on the window beside me, signaling the all-clear. "Ready?" I wait for their nods of confirmation before I firm my jaw and nod. "Let's fucking end this."

Chapter Twenty-Eight

Brielle

My heart is an unsteady machine as I slip from the backseat, the thrum of beats a disjointed melody that leaves me lightheaded and woozy. *I need to breathe.*

Rhys places a steadying arm around my waist, his green gaze studying me as we make our way toward the front door, passing the large crowd of people that are gathered outside. The masquerade turned out to be a larger draw than the brothers or I had anticipated when discussing this throughout the week, but hopefully, that will work in our favor.

"Let's get you a drink." Rhys' voice is in my ear as we walk through the foyer and take the elevators up to the second floor, completely bypassing the woman at the counter, where we'd stopped on our first journey here.

"I shouldn't. Aren't I supposed to be on alert, too?" I whisper, leaning into his side as we step off onto the second floor.

"I think we'd all prefer you to be a little tipsy than scared, Flower," he replies, nodding to Everett, who is quick to disappear toward the bar.

The room is packed full of moving bodies, and the floor vibrates with pulsing music, the beats spilling from the speakers loud enough to shake my already wobbly frame. The catwalks that had been in place during my first visit here have vanished, their missing structures replaced by a large dance floor that is crowded with swaying patrons. The waitresses, clad in exposing lingerie, bustle by in lace masks, their arms full of trays of drinks as they tend to the booths lining the walls. You'd think the sex appeal would've died down without the men and women parading around in restraints, but somehow, the room is still thick with desire, the large space surprisingly more intimate than before.

Rhys guides me into a vacant booth, and Xander paces in front of the table, his large body nearly taking up the entire walkway.

"I should be outside," Xander mutters, his long fingers gliding over the deadly metal hidden in the waistband of his jeans as if touching it will ease some of the distress tensing his shoulders.

"If he sees you waiting out there, it'll scare him off." Rhys' reminder makes Xander gnash his teeth together in anger, his muscles rippling with his pent-up rage. He's been waiting to get his hands on Lincoln since he escaped from that clearing. Will they torture him like that other man? Or will it be worse?

"Here, pet." Everett has returned, pushing a dainty glass cocktail across the table toward me. "It's a Cosmopolitan."

I have no idea what that is, but the pink liquid seems innocent enough. I pick up the glass and bring it to my lips, surprised by the tangy flavor that explodes across my tastebuds. I immediately want to request another, but I have to remember the real reason we're here. The real reason I'm here. *Bait.*

I tip back the rest of the drink, desperate for the effects of the alcohol to start working. My body is still too tight with adrenaline, and my breaths are still coming in short, uneven gasps.

"We've got you, Flower," Rhys murmurs, wrapping an arm around me and pulling me into his side. I want to leave, but the need to end this is greater than my need to run.

"I know," I whisper, watching as Xander's blue gaze cuts angrily across the room.

"White. Older. Clean," Xander puffs out the three descriptive words we received on the man Lincoln is working for before rolling his shoulders. "There are too many masked faces to see if anyone fits that description."

"So let's get a closer look," Everett replies.

"And how would you suggest we do that?" Xander barks, his large arms crossing over his broad chest.

Everett looks at me, a small smile curling up the corner of his lips. "Care for a dance, pet?"

I blink at him, unsure if I've heard him correctly. *He wants to dance?*

"Are you fucking insane? We don't know who his boss is. He could be watching us right now." Xander's hand claps down on Everett's shoulder before he can finish extending his hand toward me in offering. "No one in here is safe."

"She needs a distraction, and *we* need to see if anyone tries to approach her," Everett counters, his voice as smooth as silk. He's calm, despite the tense shoulder currently bracketed under Xander's grip.

"I don't like this." Xander shakes his head.

"I'll have you three with me to keep me safe." My voice is a soft and comforting muse that barely registers over the music. The alcohol is helping to ease my sharpest fears, and as I reach out to take Xander's large hand, the rest of my worries vanish. I'm safe as long as I'm with them.

I stand and slide out of the booth, and place my other hand in Everett's, tugging them both behind me as I lead them toward the dance floor. Rhys is trailing behind, that mischievous grin plastered on his face as we reach the edge of the crowd. They encircle me, their large bodies acting as a brick wall, trapping me in the center of them as I begin swaying to the music. The people that had been around us have backed away, knowing who the Grimm Brothers are, and wanting to steer clear of them and *me*.

"Come on, Xander." I lift his arm and twirl beneath it, making the corner of his lips twist upward before he can stop the reaction.

"Oh, fuck me," he mutters, tugging me toward him as the music begins to pick up. My body is pulsing with the beat of the bass blasting through the speakers, and playing to the beat, I turn in his grasp to press my ass back against him.

He groans, his large frame stooping down so that he can hiss against the shell of my ear, "Don't make me take you upstairs."

"What if I *want* you to take me upstairs?" I've tilted my chin up, my slitted eyes watching him through thick lashes as I roll my hips back against him again.

His tongue darts out to wet his lips, and I smirk, reaching forward to grasp at Rhys' and Everett's shirts. I tug them closer, trailing my hands down their bodies as I continue swaying to the music.

"What do you think, boys? It sounds like our woman wants to make a trip up to the fourth floor." Xander's arms are tight as they encircle my waist before he reaches up to stroke along the hollow of my throat.

I shiver, the intensity of their eyes on me, tracking me as I continue grinding back against Xander, so *thrilling*.

"We could always take a break," Rhys murmurs, reaching out to twirl his fingers around a long strand of my hair.

"We'll get you upstairs, Amour, but...I want to enjoy this first." Xander pulls me closer to him, and I smile at the warmth of him around me, reveling in the feeling of my men and the slight buzz working through my system.

As the music slows, Xander turns me in his arms so I'm pressed against his chest, and nods toward the crowd. "If we're going upstairs, we'll need to sweep the room and check in with Joe."

"On it," Everett replies, and leaning toward Rhys, calls, "I'll find Joe."

He slips away, disappearing into the throng of swaying bodies as Rhys' hand strokes down my spine. He's hesitating, his green eyes scouring my face before he flicks them up to his brother.

"I've got her." Xander's gruff confirmation makes me shiver, a swell of desire sweeping through me.

I should be on edge, or at the very least, aware of my surroundings, but I can't seem to pull my attention away from his possessive words. *I've got her.* He'd said it like a claim. A promise.

"I'll go grab our room key." Rhys stoops down and presses a gentle kiss to my cheek. "Don't have too much fun without me, Flower."

I bite my lip, my face warm with alcohol and excitement as I look up at Xander. He's watching me, his eyes sliding down my body as he pulls me tighter against him. Like this, I can feel every hard ridge of him, the muscles packed onto his frame, and the erection swelling against my belly. We stay like that, staring at each other, drinking in the sight of our bodies pressed together, even as a new, faster paced song comes on.

"*Tu es belle, mon* Amour," he murmurs.

I don't need him to translate the meaning of that for me. I blush and tug on his shirt, pulling him down toward me. I can't bring myself to care about the setting we're in, or the danger that could be surrounding us. It all melts away as our lips connect in a searing kiss.

He's not uncertain or tame, as I would have expected him to be. He's feral. His teeth tear into my bottom lip, and his tongue invades my mouth. A growl reverberates through his chest, and I gasp as his hand cups my ass, dragging my hips forward so I'm pressed against his cock.

"Beast." My surprised moan is stifled by his mouth on mine.

I claw at his chest, desperate to pull him closer as the pulse of the beat vibrates through my body. The excitement of being here with him, the pressure of tonight, the danger of being exposed, it all swells beneath my skin until I feel near to bursting. My pussy is throbbing, and I feel the peak of an orgasm drawing closer as his tongue strokes against my own. *Fuck.*

"Not yet, Amour." Xander pulls away to rest his forehead against mine, his fast breaths fanning across my cheeks. "Your orgasms are for us, and us alone. Understand?"

"Yes." I nod, leaning into his touch as he strokes a thumb across my cheek.

"Good girl," he praises, and presses his lips to my forehead. "Let's go wait by the elevators. I want to get you upstairs and under me as soon as fucking possible."

Chapter Twenty-Nine

Xander

"Let's go wait by the elevators. I want to get you upstairs and under me as soon as fucking possible."

She giggles, a light, breathy sound that travels straight to my dick, and dips her chin as the heat of her excitement settles on her face. It's there in her eyes, in the way she licks her bottom lip, and fuck if it doesn't take all my self-control not to fuck her here on the dance floor.

"Go on, now." I order her ahead of me with a nod, and take the opportunity her turned back provides to smack her ass as she passes.

She gasps, her breath catching in her throat at my abrasiveness, but her heated gaze doesn't linger long before she's turning back to the task at hand. Navigating the crowd. It seems that, somehow during our heated dance, we slipped into the center of the horde, and now, people are pushing in on us from all sides.

With her small frame, she makes quick work of cruising through the crowd, and before I realize the danger, she's slipping too far ahead of me.

"Wait, Amour!" I call out, but she can't hear me over the music blasting through the overhead speakers.

She disappears, and I curse to myself, my heart stalling in my chest. *Fuck. Fuck, fuck, fuck.* I push forward, my shoulders knocking into a few unsuspecting patrons, and turn my head, attempting to search for her in the sea of people. It isn't until I break through the large group that I spot her toward the edge of the room, her small frame dwarfed by the man hanging on her.

Is it Lincoln? His boss? Fuck!

My rage and fear boil as I storm forward, her words reaching my ears before I have the chance to intervene.

"I'm not interested, I'm here with someone." She tries to shove off his arm, which is draped around her petite shoulders, but the fucker isn't getting the picture.

"Oh, come on—"

I close the distance between us, and snap my hand out, latching onto his collar with a low growl. "What the hell do you think you're doing?"

It doesn't take more than a second to realize that it isn't Lincoln struggling beneath my hold, or his boss. This guy is young, I can see that before I've even ripped his mask off, and his curly hair is nowhere near the color we've been searching for. Instead of gray, silver, white or a greasy shade of brown, it's dyed some unnatural hue of red.

"Woah, Beast…" He holds up his hands in surrender as I tug his mask off, his wide, fear-filled eyes jumping between me and Brielle. "I'm sorry, man. I didn't realize she was with you."

"Us." The correction comes from the elevators, and my eyes dart toward Rhys and Everett, who've finally reappeared. Everett's jaw ticks, and he repeats with a hiss, "She's with us."

Rhys wraps his arms around Brielle from behind, and eyes the man in my grasp with a raised brow. "Do you have a problem with that?"

"No. No, of course not." He shakes his head and laughs nervously as I release him. "Sorry."

"You don't need to apologize to me." I shove him forward toward Brielle, and he nods, dropping his eyes to the floor.

"Sorry for bothering you."

She lifts her chin, the strength and confidence that had been missing from her when we'd arrived now radiating off her in waves. She doesn't accept his apology. She simply leans into Rhys and tucks her hand into Everetts. I grin.

"Sorry, again." He apologizes once more before scampering away.

I watch him leave. Hell, I'm about to follow the fucker when arms wrap around my waist. I look down at Brielle, and race a hand down the length of her hair, using her nearness to soothe the anger still attempting to broil over inside me.

She gives me a knowing smile and, standing on tiptoes, whispers into my ear, "Take me upstairs, Beast. Please."

Who am I to deny her request?

Chapter Thirty

Everett

I move silently through the crowd, my eyes roving over each man that I pass as I lead the way toward the elevators. I managed to slip away for a few minutes to touch base with Joe and, although hearing that there's been no movement outside leaves a mess of emotions in my chest, I'm happy to hear that the fucker isn't idiotic enough to approach our woman while she's with us. Sure, if he keeps eluding us, there's no telling how long this mess will continue, but at least, for the moment, our presence is enough to keep her safe.

I glance at Xander once we enter the elevator, and am surprised to see a small smile tugging onto his lips as Brielle strokes a finger down his chest. Despite the stress of tonight, and the fear that my plan had spurred, he's as carefree as I've seen him in years. She's good for him. She's good for *all* of us.

When the elevator opens up to the fourth floor, Brielle steps hesitantly forward, cautious, and curious. Doors, similar to a hotel, line both side of the hallways, a beacon of escape for couples, or groups of people, who're in need of a safe space to explore one another. Locker rooms, one for men, and one for women, are on either end of the halls, stocked with spare clothes, condoms, shampoo, body wash, razors, towels, and a worker who is prepared to help in any capacity necessary.

The VIP suite is in the center of the hall, closest to the elevators. Rhys slips an arm around Brielle's waist and leads her toward the door, where he thumbs the code into the keypad so he can lead her inside.

The small gasp of excitement that escapes Brielle is enough to stir my cock in my slacks.

A four-poster bed, complete with hidden hooks for bondage, sits in the center of the room, the mattress made of a smooth red leather that allows for an easy clean up. Around the room, chains, ropes, whips, floggers, and gags are displayed almost decoratively, their matching black woven leathers a pretty contrast against the light champagne walls.

There's a spanking bench, a couch, a St. Andrew's cross, and anything else a perverted mind could ask for scattered around the room. We stock it all, intent on meeting all our clientele's needs and fantasies. After all, everyone needs a safe space to explore their darker desires. *I know I sure as fuck do.*

"What is this?" Brielle has wandered toward one wall, her fingers tracing a metal rod with cuffs on either end.

Rhys chuckles, and glances toward me, a blond brow raising over his blazing green orbs, expecting me to answer.

"It's a spacer bar. It keeps your legs open." My voice is a deep rumble, the images of her strapped down and helpless below me stirring an uncontrollable hunger through my gut. She's just so beautiful when she's sweaty, panting, and begging beneath my touch. *It's almost addictive.*

She nods, her curvy frame slowly crossing through the room as she inspects the items, her innocence obvious as she curiously fingers a few of the toys. We're all watching her, hunters, stalking their prey. Our bodies are tense, and I grit my teeth, almost unable to resist the urge to pounce.

"Brielle." Xander's low voice draws her attention away from the room, his finger crooking in a silent beckon. She floats to him, her face flushed with heat, her body moving as if pulled by an imaginary magnet. Her hands trail across his arms when she reaches him, and to my surprise, he doesn't flinch at the intrusion. "Did you see anything you'd like to play with, Amour?"

She glances back toward the wall of toys, a large smile pulling onto her full lips before she glances between the three of us mischievously. "Other than my three men?"

"Fuck, Flower." Rhys groans out the curse, raking his hand through the blond waves that fall around his face. I growl, my hands clenched into fists at my sides as the urge to touch her increases, the desperation almost palpable in my veins.

Xander laughs, a light chuckle of appreciation as he reaches up to stroke through her hair, his large frame

A Rose in Darkness

engulfing her own. He doesn't look away from her as his hand wraps around the hair at the base of her neck, tugging until her throat is exposed to him. He leans down, his teeth scraping against the sensitive flesh along her carotid before he groans and pulls away, his hand remaining in her hair to keep her trapped in his hold.

"Well, brothers? Who'd like to start?"

Chapter Thirty-One

Brielle

Oh, fuck me!

A shiver races up my spine as Everett finalizes my position, trapping my last free limb with a length of black rope, so I'm held spread and naked across the mattress. Each wrist and ankle has been secured to hooks hidden within the posts of the bed, leaving my body on display for the three men circling me. With our masks off, I can see their eyes devouring every inch of exposed flesh, and I writhe as my imagination runs wild, turning their ravenous gazes into warm, probing, hungry caresses. *Fuck me.*

"We will, pet, but we're going to play with you first," Everett rumbles.

His response makes my skin flush with heat, a small wave of embarrassment settles over me as I realize I've been whispering my wanton pleas out loud. He grins at me from the foot of the bed, his arms outstretched with his hands grasping the posts that secure my legs apart. It'll never matter how many times I've been naked in front of these men. The way their eyes watch me, the way they growl for me like starved beasts, will always make it feel so new, and exciting.

"Lift your head, Flower." Rhys is leaning over me, his green gaze alight with flames as he holds up a thick, black piece of fabric. *A blindfold.* A small smile curls up the corners of my lips at the memory of our first encounter, and the blindfold he'd adorned me with back then. *I can't believe how much has changed since then.*

I lift my head off the mattress, biting into my lower lip as he ties the fabric around my eyes, leaving me blind once it's secured in place. A small hum of approval rumbles from his chest, his long fingers tracing a warm path down my cheek, across my jaw, and down my neck. He traces the spot where Xander had bitten into my skin earlier, as if appreciating the mark on my flesh, before his touch disappears and his weight recedes from the mattress. I whine at the loss of his warm touch against my skin.

"So fucking beautiful, Amour." Xander's deep growl of approval comes from beside me, and I turn toward his voice, using it as an anchor as footsteps begin moving against the carpet, the sound disorienting.

Hands touch my ankles, just above the restraints keeping me spread, and I jump, my nerves misfiring as they attempt to overcompensate for my loss in sight.

"Relax, pet. We've got you," Everett muses, his hands racing up my calves and inner thighs before dropping back down to rest at my ankles. I release the breath that had been trapped in my lungs, my body squirming involuntarily as he continues to taunt me.

Touch me!

I want to beg, the feeling of his caress against my skin more intense, more heated, when I'm forced to focus solely on his touch. When his hands move up my thighs a third time, his fingers skim the lips of my sex, and I jolt, a desperate whimper leaving the back of my throat. *I want more.*

"Please," I whimper, rolling my hips as much as the taught ropes will allow when his hands retreat to my ankles again, his fingers tracing along my tense muscles instead of exploring the place I desperately want him.

"Needy little Flower." Rhys' hushed chuckle brushes against my outstretched arm, the heat of his words landing against my skin before his tongue darts out to trace up my forearm. The erotic feeling makes me tug at my restraints, desperation clawing up my throat. *I want them.* I want them now.

Again, Everett's hands race up my legs, but this time, his fingers trace the lips of my pussy, taking the wetness that's collected there and smearing it around my clit, which he begins circling delicately.

I moan, my head lifting off the mattress as Rhys tongue continues tracing up my arm, his teeth sinking into my shoulder, before he moves lower, to caress my breast.

"Open your mouth, Amour." Xander's rumbled command comes from above me, and I'm quick to comply as his weight dips the mattress beside me.

I can almost sense his erection, the heat of his cock warming my lips before his head presses against my outstretched tongue. I groan, greedily circling my tongue around him as Everett's finger slips into my tight center, delivering the pleasure I'd been desperately seeking.

"What a good girl," Rhys praises me, the hint of a smile lifting his words before his teeth scrape against my nipple, the shocking wave of sensations shooting straight to my core. I buck beneath his and Everett's ministrations, nearly coming apart as my lips close around Xander's cock.

"Not yet, pet," Everett muses, his finger leaving me to move in slow, agonizing circles around my clit, again.

I groan around Xander, my mouth widening as my mounting pleasure and frustration drives me forward.

I move, taking him deep into my throat, before releasing him so I can trace my tongue along his length, reveling in the low growl of pleasure that escapes when I lap up the pre-cum beading along his head.

"Fuck, Amour."

I pull him back into my mouth, whining as Rhys twists my other nipple in his hand, pinching the sensitive bud as he continues licking and plucking at the other. It's overwhelming, the feeling of pleasure building deep within me, and it only grows when Everett slips his finger back into me. I cry out, my hips lifting as he curls his finger forward to press against my inner wall, stroking the hidden bundle of nerves deep within me.

Fuck!

I come, my orgasm rolling through my body so unexpectedly I can't stop my hips from bucking against the restraints, my body writhing as the mounting sensations that had driven me forward, come crashing down.

"Good, Amour," Xander murmurs, his hand stroking through my hair and wrapping it around his fist so he can take control of the pace.

Rhys' mouth disappears from my body, but his fingers continue to fondle my nipples, teasing them so they harden further beneath his touch as Everett's breath hisses against my clit. I jump, my legs attempting to squeeze together as his tongue darts out to lick the over sensitive nub, a keen cry clawing out of my throat. *Too much.* It's too much!

Everett tsks at me, his laughter warm against my swollen lips as he dips lower to drag his tongue up my center. "We're not done yet, pet. I still want more, so you'd better hold on."

More? That orgasm was so intense, I'm not sure my body can handle another one. I writhe as he drags his tongue up my folds to circle my clit, my body completely at his mercy as Xander gently guides my mouth around him. I try to focus on him, needing the distraction as Everett begins torturing my clit, but it's impossible to ignore the sensations building deep within me. Powerless against the ropes holding me open, I roll my tongue, determined to take my mounting frustration out on Xander's cock. He growls, the hand in my hair tightening when I gently scrape my teeth along his length, a low moan of approval rumbling from his chest.

I grin, moaning out a long sound of pleasure when Xander reaches the back of my throat, ensuring that the vibrations drive him mad. With my attention divided between giving and receiving pleasure, I almost don't notice the strange plastic being fitted around my nipples until they're being squeezed and forced into tight peaks beneath the contraption. *Nipple clamps.*

The realization barely registers before Everett sucks my clit into his mouth, his finger curling within me again, to send me over the edge of pleasure. I scream out, my eyes rolling to the back of my head as Xander moves his hips faster, his own pleasure peaking. He comes down my throat as I'm calming beneath Everett's delicate touch. I take every drop, lapping my tongue against his length when he pulls himself free from my mouth. He's panting, his hand stroking through my hair in appreciation as he reaches behind me to tug at the knot holding my blindfold fast.

It's bright when the thick fabric falls away, and I drop my head back against the mattress, my body spent from the orgasms that had ripped through me so explosively. My eyes scan my men, each one primed at my side, and I grin, feeling sated. I don't expect the thick growl that reverberates through the room, pricking my skin with goosebumps as my gaze catches on Rhy's moving lips, his words causing fresh desire to pool in my stomach.

"My turn."

Chapter Thirty-Two

Rhys

"My turn." My body is tight as I slip off the mattress, rounding the bed as Everett moves out of my way, allowing me to take his place at the foot of the bed, between her spread legs.

This woman is glorious. Her eyes are hooded as she watches me, the mixture of lust and exhaustion lowering them into slits as she scans my body, the intense hunger in her gaze mirrored by my own. I scan her openly, taking my time to admire her, spread out before me like a buffet inviting me to feast. Her chest rises and falls in uneven succession, causing her ample breasts to bounce enticingly, her rosy pink nipples peaked between the black clamps holding them captive. Lowering my gaze, I groan at the sight of her swollen pussy, her release having dampened her thighs and the bed below her. *She's so fucking perfect.*

I reach out and release her legs from the rope binding her, my palms rubbing away the redness left behind by the synthetic blend that had held her open for us. She mewls at my gentle caress, her head dropping back against the mattress as she revels in the feel of my palms against her skin, her lips parted on a small sigh as I trace my fingers along the curves of her legs, memorizing her.

"Rhys." She pants my name, her hands tugging at the restraints still binding her wrists. She wants me to free her but, unfortunately, what I have planned doesn't require the use of her hands.

I strip, enjoying the tortured look that furrows her brow, and climb onto the bed, gliding up her body until I'm hovering over her. She's biting her lip, her breasts pressing forward into my chest as she squirms, desperately seeking more stimulation.

"Naughty girl. Do you want more?" My lips are at her ear, my tongue darting out to lick her lobe as she shivers and nods beneath me.

"Yes. Please, Rhys," she murmurs, her voice dripping with need. I chuckle before capturing her lips with my own, the taste of her almost as addictive as the sounds of her pleasure. With my lips locked with hers, and my tongue exploring her mouth, I lift her right leg, maneuvering it so that it rests on my shoulder.

The new position easily lines up the head of my cock with her entrance, and my needy Flower notices, her hips pressing forward in an attempt to slide me inside her. I groan, unable to resist her, my hips pressing forward to give her what she wants. She squeals when I enter her, the walls of her pussy clamping around me excitedly as I push in deep, basking in the feel of her against me.

She's panting, and I break the kiss, allowing her a moment to catch her breath as I withdraw before pushing myself back in. She moans out a curse, her hips shifting to accommodate the position as I fill her.

"Fuck, Flower." She feels incredible. I pull out and enter her again, dragging out the pleasure for both of us as I reach down to caress her clit. Her eyes roll as I touch her, my cock slipping in and out of her in slow, tormenting, strokes.

"Blaze," she grits out, her hands grasping onto the ropes, tugging at them as if doing so will urge me to move faster. I want to drag this out, but her walls are already beginning to quiver around me, signaling her rising climax. I won't last once she comes.

"Tell me what you want, Flower," I murmur, nipping at her collar bone.

"More. Please. Faster." Each word is punctuated by a small moan, the heel of her free leg pushing into my ass.

"Faster, hm?" I whisper, swirling my finger around her clit as I pick up my rhythm, moving in and out of her in quick, even, strokes. "Like this, Flower?"

"Yes!" She nods, her voice a shrill whine as her body begins to shake, the orgasm building within her beginning to crest. I push faster, tipping her over the edge with a loud groan, the feeling of her pussy clamping down around me enough to drive me past my breaking point. I thrust into her once more, reveling in the feeling before it becomes too much. I pull out, my seed spilling over the mattress below us as she writhes in my hold, small mewls leaving her on panted breaths.

I pepper her leg with kisses, my hand pumping my cock through the last of my orgasm, my head resting against her knee as I watch her with a wry smile. She's so fucking beautiful, so fucking *perfect* and...she's all ours.

Chapter Thirty-Three

Brielle

My body feels gelatinous.

I force out a breath, attempting to steady my breathing as Rhys slips from the bed, that mischievous smile lighting up his beautiful face. I want to touch him. I want to touch all of them. I'm ready to curl up on this bed with their three large bodies bracketing me in place but I'm still trapped, my arms outstretched and restrained to the poles on either side of me.

Xander is sitting on the couch across from the bed, his large arms draped over the back as he relaxes, enjoying the view. It's the calmest I've ever seen him, his blue eyes warm with hunger instead of the anger that used to cloud them. He makes no move to free me, so I glance toward Rhys.

Surprisingly, he's no longer watching me, his green gaze now fixed on something across the room as he slips into his jeans. Confused, I follow his gaze, a small breath rushing from my lungs when I spot Everett perusing the wall of toys, his clothes gone. His arms move, his hands wrapping around one of the toys before he turns, muscular legs flexing, to cross back toward us. I'm not sure how my body manages, but desire flicks back to life at the sight of his erect cock, my tongue darting out to wet my dry lips. *I guess I'm not ready to be done, yet.*

"You've been such a good girl, pet," Everett muses as he rounds the bed.

He sets the toy down beside me, and reaches up to grasp the rope binding one of my wrists. With evident expertise, he works to undo the knot, freeing my right arm before moving to work on the left. In a matter of seconds, I'm free, and he's leaning across the bed to retake the toy into his hand. "Are you up for a little more fun, Brielle?"

I shiver at the sound of my name on his tongue, my head bobbing up and down as I finally have the opportunity to eye the toy. "What's that?"

He smirks but doesn't respond, choosing instead to pass the black wand to me. I look at it curiously, sitting up so that I can inspect it further. It doesn't look like much, but there are two buttons at one end, so I press them, gasping when the toy begins to vibrate in my grasp. *Oh.*

My face flushes, and I look at him meekly, understanding dawning on me. A vibrator. I'd heard my college classmates discussing these in passing, but I'd never had the opportunity to experience one. Not when I didn't have a room of my own.

"Would you like to try it, pet?" Everett's husky voice steals me from my thoughts, and I nod, my interest piqued. He laughs at my enthusiasm, and gestures for me to lie back, his hands caressing down my body as I do. The nipple clamps are still holding fast, and he tugs at the chain holding them together, sparking a fresh wave of pain and pleasure through my system.

I moan, the toy in my grasp still vibrating profusely as he hooks his hands beneath my knees and tugs me to the edge of the bed, a hungry growl leaving his throat. With him standing between my thighs like this, I can feel his erection pressing against me, making me squirm as my desire for him mounts.

"Here." Everett nods toward the toy in my grasp, his hand outstretched, but when I try to pass it to him, he shakes his head, and takes my wrist instead. He guides my hand between my legs, and when the toy brushes my clit, I jump. "Yes, pet. Just like that."

He releases my wrist, his hands moving to my hips so he can position himself at my entrance. Intrigued, I move the vibrator back to my clit, humming in pleasure as the buzzing wand begins to pulse delicious vibrations through my clit. I moan, closing my eyes as the new sensation coils desire deep in my stomach.

"Ready for me, Brielle?" Everett asks, his voice a deep rasp. I can only manage a nod, too lost in this new feeling to form any words. He chuckles, and slowly begins to slip inside me, the combined feeling of him, and the vibrator, nearly making me come off the mattress.

"Oh god!" I squeal, my legs shaking as the onslaught of sensations brings on another orgasm. I come, my pussy clamping around Everett as he pumps in and out of me, his tight grip on my hips keeping me in place. "Brass!"

"Scream for me, Brielle." He reaches between us and presses one of the buttons on the vibrators, increasing its speed. I cry out, unsure if my body can handle another orgasm.

A slew of languid mewls ease past my lips, my hips rocking to meet his thrusts. I'm panting, the vibrator pressed firmly against my clit, my entire body tense as the bomb in my gut grows more hostile, a clock beginning its countdown.

Everett growls, and roughly tugs at the nipple clamps, the bite of pain causing me to detonate. He grits his teeth, thrusting into me as my orgasm rips through my body, wringing every available ounce of pleasure out of my system in one mind-boggling experience. I'm floating, my vision a blur as Everett reaches his own climax, his cum spilling across my stomach. I breathe out, my head swimming as I slowly begin to come down from the high of euphoria that had taken over my brain. I'm limp, exhausted, and so deliciously sore, as someone's hands maneuver my body into the center of the bed. Something wipes across my pussy and stomach, ridding me of the dampness that had wet my skin, and a warm body presses into me from behind, their strong arms trapping me against their chest. I close my eyes, sighing as another warm body slips in front of me, their hands stroking through my hair.

"Beautiful, pet. Absolutely beautiful." Everett's soft voice follows me as I slip, involuntarily, off to sleep.

* * * *

Draven

It's been well over an hour since I watched those bastards steal my woman away to the fourth floor, their greedy eyes stripping her of her innocence before the elevator doors have even closed behind them. It took everything in me not to intervene, my desperation to keep her pure almost overpowering the sane piece of my brain that knows I have to stick to my plan. I can't confront them all head on. Not yet. It's far safer for me to remain in the shadows, to bide my time, for just a bit longer. I needed to be patient. She will be mine. One way, or another.

I bite back the groan of frustration that attempts to roll off my tongue, my shoulders tensing as I tuck away the phone I'd been using as an excuse to ignore the woman sitting beside me. Her blonde hair and revealing dress are almost as unappealing as the smile she keeps throwing in my direction, that slutty grin only reappearing once she notices me shifting.

"Can I buy your next round?" Her chest presses toward me, close enough that her breasts nearly touch my arm, and gestures toward my empty glass.

"Oh, no thank you. I'm not staying." I offer her a pleasant smile, attempting to remain polite, despite the disdain growing in my gut.

I flag down the waitress before she can bustle by, slip her a fifty, and stand from my seat.

"Really? I'm sure I could make it worth your time," the woman muses.

She traces her long, manicured nails up my arm and, for the thousandth time tonight, I'm grateful for the mask covering my face.

"Sorry, but I'm not interested."

I shrug out of her grasp and roll my eyes as her lips press forward in an exaggerated pout. I cross through the room before she can come up with a rebuttal, squeezing by dancing couples and drunk patrons. When I reach the elevator, I press the call button and slip my hand into my jacket pocket, procuring my room key. Waiting, I can't help but study the reflection staring back at me in the silver doors. My expensive suit is pressed to perfection, and my salt and pepper hair is gelled above the mask that obscures most of my face from view. I'm sure if one were to study me enough they'd recognize me, my public persona too large for my own good. It's what I get—what I deserve—after working so hard to become the man that I am today but, thankfully, no one would anticipate me coming to a place like this.

The elevator doors slide open, but as I'm about to step inside, I catch a glimpse of the men hovering inside the cabin. It's the youngest of the Grimm Brothers, surrounded by guards. His blond hair is a mussed tangle on top of his head, and a dumb smile plays at the corner of his lips, making me growl.

"Going down?" he asks.

He's waiting for me to step inside, but the happiness of his tone is making my heart palpitate in my chest. My Rose.

"Uh, no," I grit out, forcing a grin back onto my lips. In my haste to get upstairs, I'd pressed the wrong button. *Idiot.*

He nods, chuckling at my words. "Have a good night."

Oh, I intend to.

My eyes slide across the guards as I press the correct arrow, my shoulders straightening as the doors begin to close. All this extra precaution, for me. It's ironic, but they don't understand that, yet. No amount of security can keep me out. Not when I can erase my name from their computers, delete the security footage, and pay large stacks of cash for their employees to turn a blind eye. Snickering, I step into the cab and swipe my keycard across the pad that will grant me access to the fourth floor.

Blaze and those guards must be touching base with the remaining men downstairs. Their group of hired muscle made no attempt to blend in, so it wasn't difficult to spot them when I'd arrived. Unfortunately for them, I'm not the man on their radar. They'd been none the wiser when I'd been granted access to the building and, even now, I sat just beneath their noses. *Fools.*

When the elevator doors open up, I turn down the hall, prepared to sit in my room and wait. That is, until I spot a familiar head of waves walking in the direction of the locker rooms. The sight of her is enough to make my knees buckle, her gorgeous hair swaying over the luscious curves of her ass. She must be going to get cleaned up.

Alone.

I creep down the hall, watching as she opens the door to the women's locker room before disappearing inside. I don't have much time.

I race toward my room, unlocking the door and propping it open enough that it sits just slightly ajar. It's not open enough to catch the unsuspecting eye, but without the handle latched, it's simple to turn the knob and push inside. *Perfect. This private sex room may not be up to my standards, but so far, it seems to be working to my benefit.* Glancing toward the VIP suite, where I'm sure the other brothers are waiting, I cross back down the hall. *It's finally time.*

Chapter Thirty-Four

Brielle

I turn, checking myself in the mirror one more time, ensuring each strap is in place before I exit the locker room on unsteady legs.

That had all been so...erotic. I'd never had the chance to enjoy all three of them together, and now that I have, I'm not sure I ever want to go back. There's something so fulfilling about pleasing them all *together*. It's invigorating, and the thought alone is enough to make my stomach clench as my face heats with undeniable desire. I'm not sure how my body is still ready for the swarm of heat that sears through my veins after so many orgasms, but I lick my lips, my stomach tightening with anticipation.

I'll have to wait. While my nerves may be ready to dive back into a world of pleasure head first, my body still needs more time to recover. Washing up in the locker room had only proved how sore I'd become after my time with the three of them in that room. The thought is enough to make me giggle.

I skim my fingers along my face, feeling the heat and the smile still lingering there. I'd been anticipating their distraction when we first arrived tonight, but I hadn't imagined I'd actually feel *happiness* while on our mission tonight. But, of course, my men like to keep me on my toes, and here I am, day dreaming like a child, imagining what our future together could look like. I'm so lost in my thoughts, that I'm unprepared for the solid chest I slam into, an apology spilling from my lips as I look guiltily up at the stranger I hadn't noticed in the hallway with me.

"Well, well," he murmurs, the cobalt color of his eyes so striking against the black mask concealing his face, that I feel, for a moment, like I recognize him. "What's a Rose like you doing in such a dark place like this?"

The man's words cause the smile to fade from my face, my heart beat fluttering to a halt in my chest. Had he just...called me *Rose*?

I swallow, panic and fear shooting through my body, constricting my lungs and squeezing the air from my chest until I'm left suffocating. Wildly, I shoot my eyes toward the safe haven of the VIP suite, desperate to get back to my men. I'd left while Xander and Everett were still asleep. I hadn't thought...

"Don't be afraid," he whispers, the darkness of his tone making his docile words feel far from comforting. I take a step back, retreating under his scrutinizing gaze as a smile curls onto his lips, his cobalt eyes tracing my frame. He's moving, circling me like a predator ready to pounce, and I jump, moving with him as he turns. When he steps toward me again, I stumble backward, my spine hitting the door handle of the room behind me. I'm frozen, too paralyzed with fear as his hand reaches toward me, his fingers capturing a strand of my hair, which he twists delicately. "I won't hurt you."

"D-don't touch me," I whisper, my eyes once again racing toward the room where my men are sleeping. I want to run to them, to duck into their arms and hide beneath their power, but this man is blocking my path, his fingers still twisting my hair. He leans forward, his already impossibly close frame pressing closer as he inhales my scent, the action making blood rush through my skull. *I need to get out of here.*

Before I can think better of it, I twist the handle of the room behind me, pushing inside so quickly that I trip over the threshold. My head stings from the sudden pull to my hair, but before I have the chance to register the twinge of pain, I turn on my knees and slam the door shut, my shaking fingers forcing the lock into place.

I gasp out a choked sob when the door is closed, tears pricking my eyes. *I made it. I'm okay.* I stand on shaky legs, my eyes locked on the door in front of me. There's no struggle, no rattling handle or cursed shouts demanding that I let them inside. There's nothing. Just silence.

Did he leave?

I know better than to open the door to check, but the silence is enough to ease some of the anxiety attempting to strangle me, a signal that, despite the terrifying confrontation, he's not going to come after me. I just have to wait, now. Surely, the Grimm Brothers will come looking for me soon.

The promise of my men waiting for me doesn't stop the shakes that ripple through my body, but it does help my breath come a little easier, the promised safety of their protection allowing me to draw in a deep breath.

In the darkness of the room I've stumbled into, I take a moment, waiting until my heart rate has slowed and the shaking has eased to begin thinking about the masked stranger again. Who was he? Why hadn't he tried to follow me into this room? I turn away from the door, attempting to scan the dimly lit space as my mind races with questions. Had he meant me any harm? Or had the nickname just been a sick coincidence?

"Oh my god!" The words rush past my lips when my eyes land on the bed, and the figure standing at the foot of it. I turn back toward the door, embarrassment heating my face. "I'm so sorry, I thought this room was empty."

What do I do? I can't go back out there, but I can't stay in here, interrupting whatever's going on behind me.

There's no response from the other person in the room with me, and again, like in the hall, my skin prickles with anxiety. I peek over my shoulder, only now noticing the rope keeping them tethered in place. Are they...stuck?

"Do you need help?" I creep closer, searching for a way to release them from their bonds. It's only when I've nearly reached them that I notice a thick band of rope tied around their neck and realize, with a sickening twist of my gut, that their toes aren't touching the floor.

Gasping, I scramble back, my hands racing over the walls in a desperate attempt to find the light switch. When my fingers hit it, and the room is filled with light,

I'm almost too afraid to look up. *I have to.* What if they're alive?

Raising my eyes, I swallow back a scream, my knees wobbling beneath me. The man is hanging from the ceiling, his eyes bulging out in silent horror. I gag at the sight, bile burning my throat as I take in his slack jaw, his missing tongue, and finally…

His wolf tattoo.

I don't attempt to repress my screams now, anger and fear stirring the ungodly sound from deep within my chest. I recognize him. I know his face. I squeeze my eyes shut, vomit spilling past my lips. The man…the man that's haunted my dreams.

It's Lincoln Fisher.

Sign up for our newsletter and find out about all our romance book releases, eBook sales and promotions, sneak peeks and FREE romance books!

Want to see more from this author?
Here's a taster for you to enjoy!

The Cursed Rose:
A Rose Ever Altered
Haylynn Downing

Excerpt

Xander

Screaming.

The sound echoes through the room around me, but I don't flinch, my face a blank, uncaring slate.

Beast.

"Please, stop!" The woman screams, her words a sharp, shrill cry that breaks through my carefully curated mask. My eye twitches.

Be a Beast.

The snap of the belt rips through the room before the sting of it tearing into my raw flesh registers. It's sudden and so intense that it knocks me to my knees.

"No emotions. No sympathy." My father's harsh voice barks over the snap of another blow, the pain of it ripping into my skin punctuating his demand.

Be a Beast.

I force back the tears that threaten to form, and bite back a cry of pain as another blow hits me, striking my shoulder blades, knowing the sight of any emotions, any pain, will only increase my punishment. And her torture.

"I-I didn't know, I swear!" The woman is pleading for her life, attempting to appease my father for the crimes of her husband, who lies dead on the floor at her feet. She's bloodied, her face swinging back and forth as my father's henchman readies another blow.

"You're a liar." My father's split attention doesn't allow me a moment of reprieve. His damning words spur the henchman on, and another devastating blow crashes across the woman's face in time with the belt against my back.

She screams again but, this time, I don't flinch. I swallow my emotions, the rage, the pain, and the fear.

My father's blows stop.

I'm a Beast.

Nothing more. Never anything more.

"P-please." Her cries are weaker now as her blood pools down the front of her mangled body, staining her torso a disgusting shade of red. She's dying, but it doesn't matter. My father won't show her mercy. He shows mercy to no one.

"Are you watching, Beast?" My father laughs, reaching out and grasping my hair. He yanks, ensuring that my head remains upward and my eyes locked on the woman in front of me. Even if he weren't holding me, I'd have no choice but to watch.

I have to be a Beast.

"Yes, Father."

* * * *

I will never forget the sound of that woman's screams. Her weeping over her husband's death—the first person I ever witnessed die by my father's hand—and the guttural sounds of her demise, follow me even as I jolt out of the nightmare.

I'm tiptoeing the edge of awareness, my body still heavy with sleep, but even half-awake, I can still hear her. Her cries are sharp and loud, and they morph, blending until I realize with a shattering blow that the sound isn't just a horrible memory coming to haunt me. The screams are real. They're coming from outside of our   room. And it's Brielle.

I bolt upright, my body moving instinctually toward the sound as Everett rouses on the bed behind me, groggy. "Get security. Find Rhys. Now!"

Brielle's screams echo from somewhere down the hall, and they continue to reverberate through my skull long after they've ended, the sound buzzing through my head, striking panic with each thump of my unsteady heart.

"Brielle?" I shout, my anxiety swelling as silence settles over the hall. "Brielle!" I turn wildly, a feral roar ripping from the back of my throat as I eye each closed door, rage burning through my veins. I fell asleep. "Brielle!"

I start banging on doors, straining my ears as I listen desperately for a sound, a sign, or anything that might point me in her direction. People are filing into the hallway, confusion and curiosity stoking their interests as I continue, their murmured voices in the shallow space stoking my rage.

"Shut the fuck up!" My shout bounds down the hall, silencing the crowd that has gathered as I continue my assault on all the unopened doors.

I race down the narrow space, shoving through bystanders, and rapping on doors until finally, in the silence, I hear muffled cries.

"Brielle?" I yank at the handle, twisting the knob with what should be enough force to rip it from its frame, but it doesn't budge, worsening my panic.

"Brielle!" I kick out my leg, the heel of my foot colliding with the wood hard enough to shake the door in its frame, but still, it doesn't open. *Fuck!* "Brielle? Amour, can you hear me? Can you open the door?"

I press an ear against the wood, trying unsuccessfully to assess the situation on the other side. Is someone in there with her? Is she hurt? Is she being hurt?

The last thought has me stepping back again, my leg lifting as I prepare to deliver another hard blow to the door but, before I can kick it forward, there's the sound of a lock unbolting. I stall, eyes wide as the door cracks ajar. I move, racing forward to catch Brielle as she collapses through the doorway, a loud sob escaping her lips.

"Amour," I whisper, my hands racing over her shaking frame as I feverishly check for injuries. She's panicking, her breaths coming in short, rushed pants as the door opens further behind her, revealing the room she'd been trapped in. And the man hanging in it.

Lincoln Fisher.

Fuck.

"Clear out. Everyone, get out now!" Everett has returned, Rhys and Joe hot on his heels as he ushers away the hovering crowd, his booming demand quickly scattering the vultures.

"I've got you, Amour. It's okay, just breathe." I stroke a hand through her waves and tuck her into my chest, stepping back with her so my brothers can access the room.

"Secure this level. No one leaves the building until they've been cleared by me, understood?" Everett has taken control, his order quickly springing Joe into action as he and Rhys slip in to further inspect the space. I don't move any closer. I can see enough from here to grasp what's happened.

Lincoln got greedy.

"Xander." Brielle's voice is small and broken, her fingers digging into the fabric of my shirt. "Please, take me home. I want to go home."

I think for a moment that she's asking to go back to the house that I stole her from, but when her eyes lift to mine, I understand. She wants our home.

"Brass. Blaze," I call over her head, ensuring she stays turned away from the scene behind her as I begin tugging her down the hall. "I'm getting her out of here."

Rhys' green gaze meets mine, and his brows furrow as he glances between me and the shaking woman in my arms, a silent demand in his gaze. *Take care of her.*

I nod my understanding, my arm banding around her waist as I lead her toward the elevator, my thumb moving in small circles at her hip.

"I'd just wanted to get cleaned up. I-I didn't think…"

I'm not sure that her whispered words are meant for me to hear, but I shush her anyway, tugging her into the elevator as her teeth begin chattering uncontrollably.

"In and out, Brielle. Slow, deep breaths," I murmur gently, holding her firm against me as the elevator slowly descends the three floors.

This outcome isn't one that any of us anticipated. I'm not sure how the fucker got through our doors, or how he managed to die right under our noses, but I intend to fucking find out.

When the elevator opens on the first floor, I stoop down and lift Brielle into my arms, rushing her through the crowded foyer before the raised voices of the patrons gathered there can reach her. Rumors are already spinning, and I won't have our girl caught in the middle.

My long legs move quickly to carry us across the parking lot and to the car, my voice a low growl as I pass the remaining guards hovering around the vehicle. "Take us home."

About the Author

A mother, wife, and avid reader, Haylynn Downing grew up with an innate love of writing. In every notebook from her childhood, you can find doodles of characters and stories scribbled amongst the schoolwork that was meant to be on their pages. A resident of the Midwest, Haylynn spends her free time enjoying the ever-changing weather with her family, and creating books for her readers to enjoy. As a newly found erotica reader, it wasn't until 2020 that Haylynn discovered her passion for writing steamy, sexy romances. Now, not a day passes that new plotlines and possessive alpha males aren't taking up residence in the back of her mind, just waiting to come to life.

Haylynn loves to hear from readers. You can find her contact information, website details and author profile page at https://www.firstforromance.com

ENTWINED PUBLISHING